T. J. Richards

Shifting Scenes

Poems

T. J. Richards

Shifting Scenes
Poems

ISBN/EAN: 9783743463516

Manufactured in Europe, USA, Canada, Australia, Japa

Cover: Foto ©Andreas Hilbeck / pixelio.de

Manufactured and distributed by brebook publishing software (www.brebook.com)

T. J. Richards

Shifting Scenes

Shifting Scenes

POEMS

BY

T. J. RICHARDS

SAN FRANCISCO
THE BANCROFT COMPANY, PUBLISHERS
1889

✻

TO

MY MOTHER

This Book is Affectionately Dedicated

✻

PREFACE

Four years ago, I came to the Golden State, seeking the benefits of its " glorious climate." During a period of enforced leisure. I employed part of my time in writing verses for different papers in this State and elsewhere.

Collecting those and others I had written before, I made arrangements with A. L. Bancroft & Co. to publish them in one volume.

But with the loss of their house by fire my work was consumed just on the eve of completion ; and my first votary gift on the Altar of the Muses was a burnt offering. I now present a number of my poems in this little book, hoping they may receive whatever degree of attention and patronage their merits may demand.

THE AUTHOR.

CONTENTS

	PAGE
AFTER THE WAR	157
AFTER VACATION	36
AS LITTLE CHILDREN	20
AT THE SPRINGS—MORNING SCENE	77
AT THE SPRINGS—EVENING SCENE	79
AUTUMN LEAVES	140
BECAUSE	105
BEREAVED	121
BRASS CUT BRASS	27
CALIFORNIA VILLAGE, A	98
CARL	18
CHRISTMAS	29
CROSSING THE PLAINS	61
CROSSING THE MOUNTAINS	65
DECORATION DAY	96
EPIGRAMS	155
FLOWER, A	14
FORBIDDEN	26
FRAGMENT, A	74
GOLDEN WEDDING, A	123
I DREAMED THAT YOU LOVED ME	129
INDEPENDENCE DAY—1886	81
INDEPENDENCE DAY	108
IN THE CITY	136
IN THE MOUNTAINS	134
JENNIE ON THE BANKS OF BONNIE DOON	85
LABOR AND REST	15
L'ENVOI	164
LESSON, A	145
LETTER TO MY MOTHER, A	89
LINES IN AN ALBUM	73
LOSS	103
LAW OF LOVE, THE	119
LIFE'S POEMS	19
MAIDEN'S GRAVE, THE	63
MEMORIAL DAY	115
MISTS	139
MOTHER'S KISS, A	162

	PAGE
My Bete Noir	114
My Love	161
My Mother's Gone	130
My Native Village	37
My Neighbor	28
Not an Earthly Kingdom	107
Oh! Sing Me a Song	113
Old Schoolhouse, The	32
Only a Letter	21
O Tempores, O Mores	100
Pacific, The	67
Parted	137
Past, The	122
Perhaps 'tis Best	17
Picture, A	106
Prelude	9
Purified	138
Remembrance	93
Rest	133
Separation	83
She Must Not Know	97
Shifting Scenes	11
Song for the Times, A	120
Summer Fantasy, A	94
Summer Scene, A	141
Thanksgiving Day	24
Thoughts on Life	31
To an Absent One	160
To——	132
Two Homes	70
Two	86
Vacation Musings	147
Valley of Capay, The	156
Valley of San Joaquin, The	92
Wasted Hours	87
When My Ship Comes In	118
Within	89
World, The	71

Prelude

"WHY should you sing?" a critic said to me;
"Your fathers never sang; and can you then
Expect to pour a flood upon the world,
Whose richest note shall find a faint response
Within the human heart? From fairy groves
Enchanted, redolent with odors sweet
From tropic flowers, where waters dark
Glide noiselessly 'neath overhanging boughs,
Or catching glimpses of a radiant sun
Through rifted archways, scintillate with joy,
Comes music sweet from many a bird of song;
With beauty in its varied forms and hues
Begirt, their notes will carry the impress
Of their surroundings. So the poet, who
Would have his song touch with a moving power
The heart of the vast universe, and live
Through coming years, must in an atmosphere
Of harmony be schooled." And I replied:
"'T is said that many leagues a river may
Flow 'neath the ground; and ere we are aware
Will issue forth and make the meadows gay
With variegated hues; and so with life:
There is an undercurrent in the thoughts
Of men for ages, till some day it breaks

Into a ripple of bright song; and then
We stand and wonder that it can be thus;
And sometimes by the beaten road we hear,
From some lone warbler covered with the dust
From passing pilgrims, music rich and rare.
And may we not among the lowly find
One who may sit beside the trodden paths
Of earth, and make them resonant with song?
Much need has he of knowledge, and to feel
What other hearts have felt, and have a wide
Experience; but yet, I sometimes think
That learning can but make a greater, not
A truer poet."

Shifting Scenes

A VALLEY grand
      Filled by a band
Of gallant sons and lovely daughters;
      A river wide
      Whose currents glide
From frozen fields to sunny waters.

      A merry rune
      Of rosy June
Sung by a joyous youth and maiden;
      A pleasant stroll
      O'er dell and knoll,
Then home-returning flower-laden.

      The hum of bees
      'Neath spreading trees
That arch the murmuring streamlets over;
      Sweet songs of birds,
      The low of herds
That graze in fragrant fields of clover.

      The stifling air,
      The lightning's glare,
The mutter of the distant thunder;
      The driving blast
      Wide sweeping past,
The forest giants rent asunder.

A silvery sheen
The banks between,
The music of the brooklet stopping;
Storm-clouds unrolled
O'er field and wold,
And snowflakes dimly downward dropping.

A parting sigh,
A last good-by
To cherished friends and kindred spoken;
Love's golden chain
Drawn out amain,
But with each tender link unbroken.

A wide expanse,
A passing glance,
An ever-swaying onward motion
Unto the West
Where sinks to rest,
The red sun in the misty ocean.

Bright crowns of snow,
Dark clouds below,
A swift descent from lofty mountains;
A bursting through
The mists into
A view of sunlit fields and fountains.

A reach of plain,
Where golden grain
Glows 'neath the molten skies o'er-arching;
A night of stars
And streaming bars—
Past all the moon so stately marching.

A glimmering light
On orchards white,
And purple clusters downward bending;
The liquid tones
Of tropic zones
With Northland voices strangely blending.

A gleam of gold
In cañons old
'Neath rills from snow-capped summits flowing;
A sun-kissed vale,
A perfumed gale—
The breath of orange-blossoms blowing.

A youth unknown
Who walks alone—
A simple wreath his treasure only—
And views serene,
Each shifting scene,
Through all his devious wanderings lonely.

A Flower

CROSS the street
The busy feet
Of laughing childhood stray;
While from the bowers
Incense of flowers
Floats out each summer day.

The passers by
Will oft draw nigh
To view the happy scene;
For pictures rare
Will banish care
And make our life serene.

One only flower
Is in my bower
And few will pass this side,
And pause to see
How fair it be,
Although my joy and pride.

But yesterday
There came this way
A child with golden hair,
And asked that she
This flower might see
That seemed to her so fair.

And so I write
My verses light,
And place them humbly here ;
And it will be
A joy to me
If but one heart they cheer.

Labor and Rest

EYOND the mountain heights of Pain
There lieth Italy's fair plain ;
And who would reach that glittering prize,
So tempting unto human eyes,
Must daily strive those heights to cross,
Nor count the labor nor the loss.
The years may come, the years may go,
But still the progress will be slow ;
Though many mountains we cross o'er
Yet others ever rise before ;
And dangers we shall daily find
As great as those we leave behind.
We strive through youth and manhood's prime,
And through declining age we climb ;
Till on some mountain height we stand
And view afar the Promised Land ;

How few while toiling o'er the way
Can glean some pleasure for each day?
How few beguile a weary hour
By gazing on some wayside flower?
Or in the journey ever look
With rapture on the babbling brook,
That wanders through the valleys green
And adds new beauty to the scene.
Our thoughts are on the far away,
The glittering prize we'll win some day;
And thus we labor evermore,
With crosses here and crowns before;
Yet still methinks he toileth best,
Who in his labor findeth rest.

Perhaps 'T is Best

PERHAPS 't is best we may not know the morrow,
The weary rugged paths our feet shall tread;
The dark and unrelenting clouds of Sorrow
That in the future will hang overhead.

Perhaps 't is best that we should toil and strive;
Rest comes more sweet unto our own fireside
When to each duty we have been alive,
From morn till noon, from noon till eventide.

Perhaps 't is best the past has had its woes;
'T will fit us for the trials yet to be;
Perhaps 't is best that they should come—who knows?
Although their justice now we may not see.

Perhaps 't is best the Crown is still before.
While presses heavily each day the Cross;
We yet may know before our toils are o'er,
'T will be our gain, what now we deem our loss.

For soon with all, Life's journey will be o'er;
And we shall tread no more these paths so dim;
Perhaps 't is best before we reach that shore,
To only know—that we shall be like Him.

Carl

HE speeds along the stony street
On his bicycle, trim and neat;
My pen I drop with joy to greet
    Our little Carl.

How true he sits! how well he guides
Those noiseless wheels! how swift he rides!
Now quickly out of sight he glides—
    Our neighbor Carl.

Though lost to sight, methinks I see
Him riding onward gracefully;
So bright, so fearless, and so free—
    Our hero Carl.

With books or work or healthful play,
He well employs each passing day;
And all who know him kindly say,
    " Our noble Carl."

On you my boy and such as you,
Our land is looking to renew
Her serried ranks of patriots true—
    Our faithful Carl.

And when your youth is nobly spent,
With strong firm hands may you be sent
To turn the wheels of government—
    Our manly Carl.

Life's Poems

SOME lives are poems,
 In which we find
Words of true wisdom
 For heart and mind;

Gems of rare beauty,
 Mines of rich thought,
Lessons of duty,
 Life's problems wrought;

Full of devotion,
 Simple, yet grand,
Free as the ocean,
 Yet firm as the land.

May Life's Poems ever
 Be so pure and chaste,
That dying, we'll never
 Wish one line erased.

As Little Children

THOUGH Age may leave on form and face,
　The lasting impress of his hand,
And we may walk with faltering pace,
　That dim and shadowy border land,
Oh! may our hearts untouched by Time,
Be youthful in that darker clime.

Though centuries to cycles grow,
　And rivers still flow to the main,
When we have passed from earth we know
　We shall not tread these paths again;
Oh! then while here may our hearts be
Like those of childhood, pure and free.

If we would teach mankind the way
　That leads unto a higher plane
Of duty than they walk to-day,
　Our hearts must ever young remain;
Life's rarest charms cannot atone
For pure young hearts now older grown.

But wayworn, weary with the strife
　Where maddening passions spurn control,
How oft the cares and toils of life
　Will harden and contract the soul;
And hearts that once were light and free,
Lose their childlike simplicity.

Only a Letter

NLY a letter—faded and torn—
  And dim and yellow with age;
With here and there a leaf well worn,
  That holds some cherished page.

Only a letter—but it reveals
  The past long hid from view;
And I think to-night of a youth who kneels
  His promise to renew.

And I see the form of a maiden fair,
  Her bright eyes dimmed with tears;
And her heart acquainted with grief and care,
  Is swayed by its hopes and fears.

For love to her is a sacred theme,
  Not the jest of a passing hour;
And to awaken from its dream,
  Lies not within her power.

It gives her courage to endure;
  It speaks in her every tone;
And fills her life so young and pure,
  With a beauty all its own.

And what of him?   He says his heart
  Shall ever faithful prove;
That Death itself can never part
  Him from his life—his love.

But, oh ! he thinks to still be free
   A while to use each power ;
And like the changeful, wanton bee,
   To flit from flower to flower.

For in dreams he had seen the Ladder of Fame
   As it touched on the glowing ground ;
And his soul in rapture caught the flame
   Of the glory that shone around.

And he saw the angels of Song descend
   From their home by the crystal sea ;
And heard earth's sweetest music blend
   With their heavenly melody.

And he awakened to impart
   His lessons of Mystic Lore,
· And ope new fountains in the heart,
   Unknown, unfelt before.

All Truth, all Beauty touched his heart—
   Around, beneath, above—
His love for the maid was but a part
   Of a Universal Love.

And Love is blind; but, oh, she feels
    Despite of Love and tears—
He is untrue; his tone reveals
    Too plainly what she fears.

And a sharp pang like a poisoned dart,
    Strikes deep her womanly pride;
And she strives to check the love of her heart
    Though it swells like the ebbing tide.

Only a letter—but I can trace
    Its lines though yellow with age;
And the charm of a life's last lingering grace
    Is seen on each cherished page.

Ever cherished by him, although
    It crushed his every hope;
And left him stunned beneath the blow,
    His darkened way to grope.

He knows he well deserves the fate
    That holds them thus apart;
And he has learned—but learned too late—
    The worth of a woman's heart.

Thanksgiving Day

"TO-DAY, let all the people to
    The house of God repair;
Or in their homes with reverence due
    Lift up their hearts in prayer.

"Thank Him to-day for rich increase
    In basket and in store;
For Hope renewed; for smiling Peace,
    That comes to every door."

As points the needle to the pole,
    As rivers to the sea,
So on this day, the careworn soul
    Will turn to Heaven and Thee.

Although condemned by fate these years
    'Mid distant scenes to roam,
When this day came—in joy or tears,—
    I sought my dear loved home.

A father's blessing then I knew,
    A mother's love and prayers;
And brothers, sisters, kind and true,
    Made light my toils and cares.

To-day the glad bells joyous ring
   In tones so clear and high—
And now I hear the choir sing
   Within the church near by.

"All hail the power"—that dear old song
   Swells grandly upward there—
"Of Jesus' name"—in chorus strong,
   Floats out upon the air.

"Let angels"—fainter now each word,
   I scarce can hear them all,
Some passing breeze the air has stirred—
   "Let angels prostrate fall."

How often have I heard that hymn,
   In other days gone by,
Within a church now old and dim,
   Near where our loved ones lie.

How many cherished forms I've seen
   Pass from this earth away,
Whose memories and graves are green
   On this Thanksgiving Day

But Him I'll praise, though tears should blind
   Me as I speak His love;
Those gone before are links that bind
   Me to that Home above.

And here I've mused upon the Past,
  So far away and dim,
Until I listening hear at last
  That tender closing hymn.

And "God be with you"—Oh! how sweet
  To me that sad refrain,
As they in measured tones repeat
  Now, "Till we meet again."

He is our Father and our Friend,
  He'll guide us all the way,
Until at last in Heaven we'll spend
  One grand Thanksgiving Day.

Forbidden

IN yonder bower,
    So wild and free,
  There blooms a flower,
    But not for me.

  Its fragrance sweet
    Perfumes the air;
  How rich a treat
    To enter there!

  And oft I go
    This flower to see;
  But well I know
    'T is not for me.

Brass cut Brass

A RISING poet, not long ago
  Chanced to meet with a poet brother;
They talked of their poems for a while,
  And then about themselves and—each other.

Said one : " My poems are beautiful ;
  'Twould please you to hear me quote 'em;
But I can't remember 'em now no more
  Than if I never had wrote 'em.

" I see the poems I write sometimes,
  And I really do not know 'em ;
I read to-day one I wrote last year,
  And I thought it was Tennyson's poem."

Said the other poet so young and fair ;
  "I write not for praise nor for pelf, sir ;
But Tennyson saw my poem last week,
  And declared that he wrote it himself, sir."

My Neighbor

 SEE her as she daily goes
Intent upon her duty;
Not seeking to be known by those
Renowned for wealth or beauty.

So kind and gentle in her ways,
So plain and unassuming;
With Heaven's own celestial rays,
Her path through life illuming.

One question she has answered me;
" Is this life worth the living?"
" Yes; if for every blessing we
Some fair returns are giving.

"It is not Rank, it is not Place,
That makes our lives respected;
The highest station brings disgrace
When Duty is neglected.

"Trust Him unto the utmost, through
Each dark and trying hour;
But still know we must ever do
What lies within our power."

These lessons, fair one, learned from you,
New faith and hope have brought me;
But not by words, but actions true,
Their cherished truths were taught me.

When Merit only, shall be Rank,
And Beauty—love and labor,
For such a blessing I will thank
Kind Heaven—and my neighbor.

Christmas

CHRISTMAS comes! "Peace and goodwill
On earth to all mankind."
Though years have passed that message still
Revives each heart and mind.

Blest Day! What joy clusters round
Thy name! The hours we knew
Long past of happiness profound,
Come once again to view.

Now round our hearthstone we shall meet,
And friends will gather there—
Bright cheering words our hearts shall greet
And banish pain and care,

And though without the wintry blast
  Is blowing shrill and drear,
Within our home, no clouds o'ercast
  Our Merry Christmas Cheer.

While happiness shall fill each breast
  In this, our dear loved home,
Oh! may our love go out in quest
  Of those who sadly roam.

But there are many friends of yore
  Still held by us most dear,
Who'll never greet our coming more
  When Christmas shall appear.

Christmas comes! Now open wide
  The portals of the heart;
Forth let the dove of Mercy glide,
  Its message to impart.

And while of Peace the angels sing,
  May Earth catch the refrain;
Till Hate shall lose its deadly sting
  And Charity shall reign.

And Faith and Hope, her sisters, then
  Will follow at her call;
And Christmas need not come again
  To teach us love for all.

Thoughts on Life

A HUMBLE lot is mine to-day;
A lowly path I daily tread;
And yet I know this lowly way
To higher planes of life has led.

A noble lesson we have learned,
When we can curb Ambition's lust,
And rightly prize the place we've earned,
Nor seek, nor shun a higher trust.

And what though Merit often fail
And yield the crown to Birth or Fate!
None need Misfortune's lot bewail;
They yet shall reign who patient, wait.

A wild bird sang—none heard but me;
And yet its song was full as sweet
As that within yon maple tree
That stands beside the crowded street.

But oft we keep our brightest smile,
And kindliest word, and fairest song,
That would some trusting heart beguile,
And save them for the idle throng.

A kindly greeting we refuse
The lowly ones we daily meet;
And grasping at the stars, we lose
The jewels lying near our feet.

But though it never may be mine
To leave behind an envied name,
Yet still I trust, I'll ne'er repine
And idly sigh for Wealth and Fame.

The Old Schoolhouse

I VIEW once more that sacred spot
Where first I trod in Wisdom's way;
The place where learned sages taught
The children of a bygone day.

I thought I would my steps retrace,
And one more look upon it cast;
And I would take from this loved place,
Some fond memento of the past.

For dearer now unto my heart
The relics of my childhood's days,
Than glimpse of classic works of Art,
Long hidden from the raptured gaze.

And I had thought to find them now,
    As when I left them years ago;
When Hope was young, and on my brow,
    I felt the flames of Ardor glow.

For I had wandered far away,
    And left the home I loved so well;
But now I had returned to-day,
    And hoped by this loved spot to dwell.

But Time had passed; and it will leave
    Its marks of progress on us all;
Its strong hand will the mountains cleave,
    And by its touch fair temples fall.

Whilst traveling in a distant land,
    Thoughts of the past come o'er our mind;
Bright visions of the broken band—
    The happy scenes we've left behind.

We backward cast our eyes the while—
    And through the intervening years,
And many a long and weary mile—
    The oasis of home appears.

We then return to that fair land,
    No more from childhood's scenes to roam;
And after years have passed, we stand
    A stranger in our native home.

No more we see a father's face;
   Nor mother's; brothers, sisters—all,
Long since abandoned that dear place
   And left but a deserted hall.

'T was thus with me. I thought while here
   Some tokens of my youth to find;
But they have vanished—year by year—
   Till scarc a trace remains behind.

I think of other days gone by,
   As I stand fondly gazing here,
And oft I check the rising sigh;
   But Memory claims and takes—a tear.

Where are my school-companions gay
   That formed that happy, youthful band?
Some long since passed from earth away,
   And some are in a distant land,

Far, far from home! and mountain height,
   And ocean billows come between;
No more their smiling faces light,
   The gloomy sadness of this scene.

And " Caledonia, stern and wild,"
   Is now the home of two fair maids,
Whose cheerful presence once beguiled
   The passing hours, in these dim shades.

Some on the fair Pacific Slope,
    Now dwell with Peace and Plenty blest,
And base their earnest Faith and Hope,
    Upon the great, and growing West.

Some far from home have perished, when
    They saw their sky with clouds o'ercast;
And one has gone—and come again—
    To muse in silence o'er the Past.

The spreading oak with branches wide,
    That cast around a pleasant shade—
How oft have I stood by its side!
    How often in its shadow played!

It, too, has left this once fair scene!
    It met a sad, untimely fate,
Its leaves are scattered on the green,
    And all around is desolate!

Oh! this act will man's folly crown!
    It fell beneath the tyrant's sway;
And vandals tore the building down,
    And Time was cheated of his prey.

Where schoolgirls' songs rang through the wood,
    The birds now sing their notes instead;
Wild flowers are blooming where it stood,
    And all its former joys are fled.

I cross again the little brook,
  As night's dark shades succeed the day ;
I turn and take a parting look,
  And then in sadness—walk away.

After Vacation

BACK from the seaside and mountains,
  Back from the health-giving spring;
From the deep-sounding sea and bright fountains,
  To our labor new life we will bring.

The birds and the brooklets awaking
  Have sung of their tenderest themes ;
And first on our rapt senses breaking
  Fair visions that came in our dreams.

Seeking the while for the pleasures
  Unburdened Existence can yield,
We have gathered the rarest of treasures
  From many an oft garnered field.

From the North where the summer belated
  Awhile on the drear landscape smiles ;
From the South where the breezes are freighted
  With odors from tropical isles ;

From the East, the germ of the Nation,
  With its glorious deeds of the Past;
From the West with its civilization,
  The grandest, the best, and the last;

From journeys in far distant nations,
  From musings 'mid Nature and Art,
We bring to our daily vocations
  A larger and kindlier heart.

With the loss of that narrow contraction
  That would dwarf and disfigure the soul,
And feeling we are but a fraction
  Of a great and harmonious Whole.

My Native Village

HERE once the woodland far extended spread,
And the wild deer her fawns unfearing led;

Where strange bright flowers in wild profusion grew,
And o'er the scene a veil of beauty threw;

Where once the squirrel with the leaflet played
And the shy rabbit sported in the shade;

Where Nature once held undisputed sway,
The works of man—fair homes—arise to-day.

Before the sturdy ax the forest fell;
The deer affrighted left its native dell;

The flowers faded 'neath the sun's bright glow,
Or lingered only by the streamlet's flow;

The tree that held the squirrel's nest of leaves
To-day supports the wide protecting eaves;

Where the Red Hunter sought the cooling spring,
We now may hear the anvil's daily ring;

The little brook that flowed adown the hill,
Turns the great wheels of yonder busy mill;

The hum of voices and the tread of feet
Are heard each day along its shaded street.

And though our village is so far remote
From crowded cities or from towns of note,

Yet still our "leading men" are all intent
On keeping pace with every great event.

From far around to hear the latest news,
The sturdy farmers come, and give their views,

In language more stentorian than ornate,
On questions of vast import to the State,

And ever and anon a contest hold
With varied specimens from field and fold;

And those who once did conquer or did yield
In other days on many a hard fought field,

Now with a rivalry far nobler, vie
In peaceful products of our sunny sky.

I look around me, thankful that to-day,
O'er all our land. Peace holds her gentle sway;

For War's grim memories now no more we hoard;
To ploughshares we have changed the rusting sword,

To tuneful anvils, balls that fiercely met;
To reaper's blades, the vengeful bayonet;

And with renewed devotion now we claim
One flag, one country, and one common aim.

Now once again the Pen resumes its sway,
And solves the problems of the passing day.

May it no more by Sordid Gain debased,
Here pander to an oft perverted taste;

Nor yield supine to Concentrated Power,
The living, vital issues of the Hour;

But toiling for a brighter, better day,
Point up to higher realms and lead the way.

When Summer smiling, sheds her glories 'round,
And dale and hilltop are with verdure crowned,

Upon our streets the village band appears,
And strains of martial music greet our ears;

While lovely maids, fair as a Morn in May,
Add beauty to the scene and throng the way;

And when the shades of Night have gathered round,
And wrapt the land in darkness all profound,

From vine-sequestered cot, or mansion white,
Borne on soft breezes through the stilly night,

Comes music sweet from some light-toned guitar,
Touched by as dark-eyed damsels as afar

In Spain's provincial towns, the traveler sees,
Beneath the groves of fragrant orange trees;

As noon and evening make their daily round,
Along the streets is heard the merry sound

Of happy children just released from school,
No longer anxious to observe "the rule."

The teacher, firm but gentle, walks behind,
With mind well stored with lore of various kind—

Skilled in each art to guide the wayward youth,
Along the path of Learning and of Truth;

But wearied with the cares that come to those
In whom the welfare of young hearts repose,

He seeks his room to gain relief from toil,
Then takes his books and "burns the midnight oil;"

And oft he dreams of a bright future, when
Instead of children, he shall govern men.

When in obedience to his country's calls
His voice is heard in Legislative Halls.

Behold where yonder lofty spires arise,
Like Faith still pointing upward to the skies!

And teaching man to look not always down
On earthly scenes, but upward to a crown,

Reserved for all who do, as best they can,
The duties that they owe to God and man.

The Sabbath dawns : throughout these quiet vales,
The songs of birds are borne upon the gales ;

Bright blooming flowers, the gently waving trees,
The low of distant herds, the hum of bees,

The tinkling bell upon the village green,
The shimmering waters in the distance seen—

Sights that we love to see and sounds to hear,
Now greet the eye and fall upon the ear.

There low, dark belts of woodland fringe the west,
Where squirrels fearless sport around their nest;

And on the south, broad pastures stretch away,
Where graze the flocks through the long summer day;

While on the north the rock-ribbed hills arise,
Whose summits glisten 'neath the glowing skies.

Far to the east, as far as eye can see,
Reach fertile prairies; where once wild and free

The antlered deer o'er it were wont to roam,
Now ruled by man—earth's storehouse and his home.

On every side fair works of art we meet,
While nature's jewels lie about our feet;

While overhead the dome of azure blue,
Now slowly changes to a deeper hue.

As high and higher mounts the King of Day,
I see the gathering people wend their way

Unto the church, nor wait until the hour
The bell shall call them, ringing from the tower.

And saints, grown old in service, come, nor fear
The idler's jesting, nor the scoffer's sneer.

Blest spirits! When at last you hear the call
To leave these scenes, oh! may your mantles fall,

As you ascend in chariots of flame,
On sons and daughters worthy of your name.

And brightly smiling maidens here are seen,
Like flowers blooming withered boughs between;

And matrons pale, whose sable robes betray
The shadows resting on their homes to-day.

And there he stands who leads, and long has led
His people in the paths their feet should tread;

And seeking for their hearts surcease from strife,
Breaks for their hungry souls the Bread of Life.

But since an abler mind in other days,
In gentler, sweeter strains has sung thy praise,

I should not try, a bard of weaker mold,
To tell again what has so well been told.

Yet will these precious memories round me throng
And swell the feeble measure of my song.

I see him now, a man of gracious mien,
'Mid every trial, peaceful and serene ;

As is some mighty current, deep and wide,
That calmly flows through Ocean's swelling tide ;

And though the darkened waves may sweep around,
Keeps ever on its way in peace profound :

He moves amid his flock with gentle pace,
And looks with kindness in each well-known face ;

Cheers the sad heart crushed by Affliction's rod,
And leads the wanderer back to Heaven and God.

Well I remember as these lines I write,
When first my fancy took its wayward flight ;

When first I ventured feebly to address
The people through the medium of the press.

I fondly thought—a childish thought I know,
I have outlived such visions long ago—

The world was waiting eager for my song,
And deemed its music was delayed too long.

How grand it looked in print!   How well it read !
And thoughts of Fame and Fortune filled my head.

I did not know, as I have known since then,
The cold and heartless apathy of men;

That of the throng that plume for lofty flights,
But few shall ever reach those dizzy heights;

That royal natures that deserve a throne,
Oft go through life unnoticed and unknown.

Perhaps 'tis best; the sweetest flowers grow
Not on the mountains, but in vales below;

They bloom in beauty in each lowly bed,
Nor feel the storms that sweep far over head;

And though oft crushed by man, their fragrance rare,
More richly rises to perfume the air.

Within these realms could we expect to find
That subtle power which sways the heart and mind,

And wakes the soul that sleeps in fatal ease
To grand and noble deeds?   Of such as these

The scholar reads in legendary lays
That tell of elder and of better days;

In records dim of ancient Greece and Rome,
Nor thinks to find true eloquence at home;

The flowers to-day are just as bright and fair
As those of other times; the New World's air

Wafts on its every breeze perfumes as sweet,
As varied and as prized as ever greet

The tastes refined of those who dwell at ease
Beside the Tigris and the Euphrates.

And why should Eloquence, sublimest art,
In this our day and clime, fail to impart

Its lessons true? Why should there be denied
These quiet scenes, man's highest, noblest pride?

No! Eloquence shall live throughout all time
Uncircumscribed by age, or race, or clime.

And it is here; we've listened to its voice;
Its power divine has made us oft rejoice;

It touched our conscience like a fiery dart,
And waked each smoldering passion of the heart.

I could not—would not—blot from memory's page,
His thoughts so worthy of a better age.

Nor soon forget that grand and noble face,
That manly form and more than manly grace;

The raptured throng each deep emotion stirred,
Hang tremulous upon his every word,

Forgetting as those magic tones they hear,
The one dark shadow of his bright career.

Though dear be Music, Eloquence, and Art,
Their power combined can never move the heart,

And keep its life blood flowing free and warm,
Like kindly deeds that patient hands perform ;

And these the skilled physician, tried and true,
Though often baffled, fails not to renew ;

Bends with compassion o'er the sufferer's bed
Till the last flickering ray of life has fled.

I see him toiling on, from day to day,
Through sun and storm on his unwearied way ;

For eager, anxious hearts his coming wait,
In humble cot, or mansion of the great,

Where trembles now, the quivering, fleeting breath,
In the poised balance betwixt life and death.

He comes! Ah! well they know that measured pace;
And with what tearful eyes they scan his face,

Long furrowed o'er with lines of wasting care,
If by perchance his thoughts are written there;

And hope against all hope, his presence near,
May turn aside the Shadow, all men fear.

Our lovely village owes thee, friend, to-day,
A debt of gratitude we cannot pay;

My feeble pen but feebly has expressed,
How much thy kindly deeds and words have blessed

Our hearts and homes; but yet despite the power
Of the warm sunshine, every blooming flower

Must fade away too soon before our sight,
Cut down by hoary frost or withering blight;

The floods of springtime may be safely passed,
The summer's scorching heat, the autumn's blast

We may survive; but yet dread winter will
The feeble current of our being chill.

Too well we know man's power cannot save
Our loved ones ever from the silent grave.

I should not mention these and fail to speak
Of those in humbler spheres, who daily seek

By honest, faithful labor, to provide
A cheerful home, where by their own fireside

May gather when their daily tasks are o'er,
And drifting snows are piled against the door,

And wintry winds are blowing shrill and cold,
Each dear, loved member of their own household;

Upon the hearth how ruddy glows the fire
When near it gather children, mother, sire!

The warring elements may close it round;
Within that home—Love, Hope, and Peace are found.

Of voice well modulated, justly proud,
One of its members deigns to read aloud

The village paper with its weekly news;
Its lovelorn verses from some unfledged muse;

Its correspondents with a Latin name—
Young seekers after literary fame;

Of how a noted wedding had occurred
Within "our town," of which they long had heard;

Of how the bridegroom looked so "very grand,"
"And is quite wealthy so we understand;"

Of how the bride a loving wife will make;
And how the editor received some cake;

Of murders, suicides,—a record dire,—
Of loss of worldly goods by flood or fire;

Of latest news across the ocean far
Predicting soon a European war.

Thanks to the Press! No more to us denied
The busy doings of the world outside;

Though never from our fireside we may stray
In foreign lands to trace our weary way,

For us the wires encircling every zone,
Soon make the deeds of distant nations known.

At last when laid aside the well-conned page,
Some simple games the youthful mind engage;

More loved and lovely now than when a bride,
From her light task the mother turns aside;

And on her face a sweet and tender smile
Dispels the gloom that shadowed it the while,

As she looks round with pride and pleasure there
On the rich treasures trusted to her care ;

And feels her toils grow lighter day by day,
When borne for those who honor and obey.

Such homes as these preserve our Nation still
From all the gathering storms of direst ill ;

Their memory lives throughout our after lives
And all the wreck of fondest hopes survives ;

Such homes produced—with pride each true heart learns,
In England, Wordsworth, and in Scotland, Burns ;

And in the New World, plain, sincere and grand,
The Lincoln and the Stephens of our land.

Perhaps within that circle thus obscure,
Is one whose thoughts for ages shall endure,

In manly prose or words of glowing rhyme,
The carps of critics and the tests of time.

Oft have I wandered by yon winding stream
And watched the softened rays of sunlight gleam

Through overhanging boughs, that turned aside
The fiercer currents of its golden tide ;

And sitting there upon a mossy bank
' Neath a majestic oak that deeply drank

The placid waters, I would watch for hours,
The many plumaged birds, the forest flowers,

The strange fantastic forms of shrub and tree,
Until some fairy scene it seemed to me,

Where magic wands, moved by some master hand,
Created cities fair and castles grand,

And peopled them with dwarfs and giants grim,
That passed before me in the shadows dim.

And here I come again before I go,
To muse alone, and watch the steady flow

Of these dark waters, that through every day,
Are nearing the great ocean, far away;

And musing thus, I think upon the time,
When thoughts of mine that flow in simple rhyme,

Shall with a deeper meaning far be fraught,
And mingle in the sea of human thought.

And there upon the rippling waves afloat
Before me passes now a tiny boat;

And on its side I see the name of one
I knew, ere yet her maiden-life begun :

Known and beloved o'er all the country side,
A mother's treasure and a father's pride;

But once as flowers fair adorned the dale,
Across the river came the boatman pale;

And in the close of that long summer day,
From home and friends he beckoned her away ;

She saw his bark approach the mist-wreathed shore,
And heard the dipping of his muffled oar;

She caught a gleaming of the shadowy sail
That slowly swayed before the phantom gale ;

Then with a look that ever seemed to say,
"Farewell, dear friends : in realms of perfect day

I'll meet you soon," she vanished from our sight,
And all our sunshine changed to deepest night;

Her voice has died from stairway and from hall;
Her form has passed beyond our fond recall ;

But what she was to us, and might have been,
Are sad, sweet memories, no fair gift may win ;

And as to-day I look upon her name,
Her memory will a passing tribute claim.

Fair as thy past has been yet still I see,
A brighter, grander future yet for thee;

When shall be heard the iron horse afar,
Approaching with the heavy laden car;

And his loud neighing wafted on the gales,
Shall wake the echoes of thy quiet vales;

When temples reared to Science and to Art
Upon these hills, their classic Lore impart;

Till from their halls, some hand reserved by fate,
Though darkened waves shall guide the Ship of State;

When men shall come from distant realms each year,
And seek new homes, and seeking—find them here;

When honest freemen shall around thee draw
The safeguards of a higher, better law.

Prosperity has richly blessed thy past,
And but few shadows have been o'er thee cast;

From War and Pestilence thou hast been free,
While some were wrapt in grief; on thee

Nor flood nor fire fiend yet have left their trace,
Nor sudden tempest marred thy lovely face ;

But Peace and Plenty smiled each passing year
And filled thy homes with love and cheer ;

Thy people, toiling on their fertile lands,
Have reaped the honest labor of their hands,

Nor feared the profits from each small estate,
Must go to swell the coffers of the great.

Thou hast thy evils too ; though far away
From scenes where Vice holds undisputed sway,—

And greedy Avarice ever lies in wait
To pluck the weak that come within her gate,

And willing victims follow in the train
Of foolish Fashion and applaud her reign—

All is not perfect here ; nor shall we find
From Folly free, the wisest of mankind.

The village apes the town ; too oft we see
They differ not in kind, but in degree.

With all thy faults, and they are many, yet
I leave thee with a deep unfeigned regret ;

And scarcely hoping I shall ever find
In all my travels, friends as true and kind,

As tried and faithful through each passing year,
As in the past I've known and trusted here;

Who wished me well, and gave me timely aid
And for my welfare worked as well as prayed;

Looked with compassion on my wayward ways,
And gave for earnest effort, earnest praise;

Nor deemed as wholly idle or as vain,
The wild and weird vagaries of my brain;

For strange poetic visions on me wrought,
And made me oft to be what I would not—

A child of Fancy striving to express
To other thoughts I hardly dared confess;

Thoughts uncongenial to the din and rush
Of busy Trade; more suited to the hush

And quiet of some calm sequestered vale,
Where Commerce spreads not to the passing gale

Her broad white wings; nor passing interests clash
Nor glittering gewgaws in the sunlight flash:

But where the gentle and refreshing breeze
Sweet music wafts through blossom-laden trees;

Where morning fair reveals to eye and ear,
Views that delight and sounds we love to hear;

Where all the passing day a varied scene
Of broad fair field and woodlands dark between,

Breaks ever on the glad enraptured view,
Each day unchanged, and yet forever new;

With friendly call from neighbor o'er the way,
Who stops in passing but consents to stay
And talk upon the topics of the day;

Till evening comes at length, and calm repose
Brings each days scenes and labors to a close;

Nor feverish dreams of Fame nor unjust Gain
Impede the flights of the fantastic brain

Into Elysian worlds of joy and bliss,
Beyond the sordid toils and cares of this:

Thus had I hoped to live, and thus to spend
The passing years, till time for me should end,

And Angel hands should beckon me away
From earthly scenes to realms of perfect day.

It cannot be; but it may be the best
That we should labor when we fain would rest;

That still the barriers firm must ever stay
That rise in silence round our narrow way;

That it lies not witnin our humble sphere
To choose the paths that we would tread while here;

For some that but in peaceful ways delight
Must wield the sword, the foremost in the fight;

And men whose hearts love but the quiet shore,
Guide storm-tossed vessels 'mid the ocean's roar;

And many follow, who were born to lead,
Deferred and scanty praise their only meed.

And we are not what we would be; each day
There is a guiding power we must obey,

That leads us into paths we would not choose,   [bruise
Where rude thorns pierce us, and where rough stones

Our weary feet; but still though tempests frown,
Our hopes are not destroyed though oft cast down;

At last we feel as we securely stand,
It was a loving though a chastening hand.

Now to the Sunset State I wend my way,
Amid its wonders for a while to stray;

To stand upon the mountain's rugged side
And look upon the fertile valleys wide;

To view the greatness of the Farther West,
Its arts and customs, and that wild unrest

That ruled so fiercely in the Days of Gold,
Nor even yet has quite released its hold.

There shall I meet again in that fair land
With members of a once united band,

Now widely sundered; but who still retain
Amid these latter days of Greed and Gain,

A deep abiding love for that dear place
Where first they looked into a mother's face;

And where their youth and mine were richly blessed
By a devoted father, gone to rest;

Whose life below was simple yet sincere;
Whose kindly deeds illumed his humble sphere;

We learned too late to prize him; but we know
He loved us; and that cheering thought shall **go**

With us through life; but oh! the pure and good
While with us, are too little understood;

Too late we grieve when they are called away
O'er unkind words and deeds; but yet we may

In future strive with constant heart and mind
To prize still more the dear ones left behind;

And when I come—if I should come again—
Relieved by milder climes from lingering pain,

I hope to smooth the last declining years
Of her who ever shared my hopes and fears.

Though dark or hopeful be my future, yet,
Friends of my youth, I shall not soon forget

Your welcome cheers whenever I prevailed,
Your tender words of comfort when I failed;

And though 'mid distant scenes my footsteps stray,
Fair village, still throughout each passing day,

My heart shall turn wherever I may roam,
To thee my earliest and my dearest home.

Oh! may thy sky be ever bright and clear,
And may thy course be onward through each year;

May Education guide thee, by her light,
And keep thee in the path of Truth and Right;

Oh! may no Goldsmith at some future day
Muse o'er thy fall and write thy sad decay;

But evermore still be our joy and pride,
And shed thy many blessings far and wide.

Crossing the Plains

I HOLD it tame to glide across
    In this fair palace these vast plains;
For greater speed is greater loss,
    And beauty less with lesser pains.

No more the rude wigwam is nigh;
    No more the dark and rolling seas
Of buffaloes come sweeping by;
    Less royal sights our eyes must please.

No more the camp-fires briskly burn,
  Nor trusty hearts stand sentinel,
And through the night with deep concern,
  Guard sleeping comrades, long and well.

But now each step is blazoned o'er
  With man's inventive daring skill;
His cities greet us evermore,
  His cattle graze on every hill.

Far to the East the King of Day
  Is rising; he has risen long
On scenes I leave so far away,
  I deem it but an idle song.

And thus each year the currents sweep;
  And so our course of being runs,
If we should wake or we should sleep,
  From rising unto setting suns.

I feel like one who sits and sees
  In some theater, far away,
Fair pictures; and I know that these
  Are preludes to the coming play.

The Maiden's Grave

ONCE in the dim and distant past
  You turned your face unto the West;
  And stopping here awhile to rest,
Found this repose to be your last.

Awhile your sorrowing friends delayed,
  Then left you here to sleep alone,
  With but a rude unsculptured stone
Above your sleeping form, fair maid.

But now a fitting monument
  Reared by true hearts that knew you not,
  Marks this sad, dreary, lonely spot
Where your last hours on earth were spent.

Fair daughter of my own fair State!
  Oh! peaceful may your slumbers be;
  Your eyes were closed ere they should see
That land for which I watch and wait.

And I, too, may not reach that shore
  Where rivers run through sands of gold;
  But from some mount, like one of Old,
I may but "view the landscape o'er."

If such my fate should chance to be,
Though friends may shed a few, brief tears,
I could not hope in after years
The passing throng would honor me.

But not to you, my heart suspects,
Alone was reared this monument;
Man in this tribute here has blent
Respect and love for all your sex.

And as I leave you all alone,
Beside the one to friends so dear,
Another monument I rear
To other hearts than I have known.

Crossing the Mountains

NOW high and higher we ascend
    This grand and lofty mountain range,
Whose snowy peaks in darkness blend
    With hovering clouds. How vast the change!
The hills and dales and woodlands green,
    And fertile prairies dotted o'er
With thriving towns—a varied scene
    That passed our charmèd gaze before—
We leave behind, and sterner sights
    Now take the place of visions fair.
We upward look to higher heights,
    And see the eagle soaring there,
Calm and serene, as if his flights
    Where native to these realms where man
Feels deep oppression, and he fears
    Though bearing up as best he can
He leaves too far his native spheres.
    And yet man ever feels a pride
That he has chanced to stand upon—
    A feat that some in vain have tried—
The topmost summit of Mount Blanc.

Around him whirls the blinding snow,
That ever threatens him with death,
And weary travelers far below,
Look up with envy, while their breath
Can scarce avail them now to stand
Upon the rugged mountain side.
Yet will they sigh for regions grand,
To them forevermore denied.

Far rather would I stay below
In lovely vales, with trees and flowers,
Than stand on mountain heights and know
That for a few brief fleeting hours,
The throng beneath were envying me—
And some were looking up with hate
And longings vain, and few there be
Would wish for me a happy fate.
Nor to the dizzy heights of Fame
Would I ascend; but rather stay
Below forever, though my name
Should with my spirit pass away.

The Pacific

FAR from my humble home beside the broad,
Majestic inland river of our land,
Across the arid wastes of deserts drear,
And over lofty mountains shutting out
Bright views of El Dorado, I had come,
Till now I stand in solemn awe beside
The waters of this mighty Sea that marks
The western confines of a continent.

I see the white winged birds of commerce now,
Swift sailing out to other shores than ours;
And in the distance, braving every wind
That fans the seas, is our fair country's flag;
Still may it float, though tempest rudely blow,
And foam-capped billows threaten to engulf
Its starry folds—the last to greet our view,
When we shall turn our steps to foreign realms,
The first to welcome us when we return.
The waves come sweeping in upon the shore
And break in clouds of spray about my feet;
And as they backward glide the children come
And gather up the shells of varied hues,
Borne landward on the bosom of the tide.

It plays before me now with tender grace
As though it never cast upon the shore '
The wreck of an Armada.
Standing here, I muse upon the time,
When turning from the countless treasures poured
Into Hispania's lap, her daring son,
Balboa, crossed the heights and saw beyond,
With joy, this crystal sea before him spread.
And marching into it with sword in hand,
There in the name of his loved king and queen,
He took possession; and with lusty arm
Upraised, vowed to maintain against all foes,
Be they his brethren in the one true faith,
Or hated infidel, this mighty claim.

And change-producing centuries since then
Have swept o'er land and sea; and thy fair shores
Have been the scenes of wasting wars; but now,
Men speaking various tongues dwell here in peace;
While through the Golden Gate is sweeping in,
On ships of stately mold, the far-famed wealth
Of Indus, which of Eld, Columbus sought.

Midway between the summit of the cliff
And its firm base the swarthy fisher stands,
And casts his line into the vasty deep,
And patient waits the fruit of all his toils.

The dashing foam breaks o'er him ; and around
The curlews screaming fly ; and far above
The ceaseless moaning of the waves is heard
The sea-lion's plaintive call.

Now as I gaze upon this restless sea,
The gray mists like a heavy curtain rise;
And I can stand and see to where there seems
A barrier that shuts from out my view,
The golden visions lying far beyond.

And so I often think is Life : the veil
Is sometimes lifted, and our eyes can see
The while into the future ; but there still
Is a vast space that we would seek to pierce,
Shut out forever, and we look in vain.
Now as I go in silence from this scene
That I may not in future view again,
My heart shall think in coming days upon
This mighty Ocean, as a type though faint
Of vast Eternity that stretches far
Beyond the dark and silent shores of Time.

Two Homes

 MODERN mansion—fair and tall,
With pictures rare upon the wall,
And many a brilliant-lighted hall—
    This is my home.

Rich music floats upon the air
And drives away each pressing care—
Oh! could there be a spot more fair,
    Than this my home.

In the far distance, mountains blue
Rise ever on the raptured view,
And add new grace and beauty to
    This lovely home.

And though November breezes blow,
They bring no chilling hail or snow,
But perfumes from bright flowers that grow
    Around my home.

*   *   *   *   *   *   *   *

A house with low moss-covered eaves
On which each blast of autumn weaves
A coronet of golden leaves—
    That was my home.

No frescoed walls nor paintings rare,
Nor parlors filled with taste and care,
Nor stainèd glass nor winding stair
  In that old home.

And yet my heart goes back each day
Along Life's weary rugged way,
To that dim cottage; and I say,
  "Here is my home."

Sweet memories of the Long Ago
Round it a veil of beauty throw,
And Fancy adds a brighter glow
  To this dear home.

The World

THE world, you say, seems cold to-day
  And denies you its pleasures sweet;
But in coming days if you win its praise
  It will cast its crowns at your feet.

It smiles on none before they have won
  The prize they have long had in view;
And a promise to pay will not win your way
  For it's older and wiser than you.

Toil on through the years 'mid trials and tears
  And the shadows will vanish away,
And your weary feet stand on mountain tops grand,
  In regions of jubilant day.

The world will outpour its costliest store
  If you've treasures to spare of your own ;
And when you shall reign o'er a princely domain,
  It will build you a radiant throne.

Oh ! then, it will smile upon you the while,
  And 'mid its fair honors you'll live,
But the love that can bless the heart's loneliness
  Is not in its power to give.

Lines in an Album

YOU ask for some lines for these pages;
   What kind would you value most, pray?
A story of long vanished ages,
   Or one of our own present day?

Shall I tell you of woman's devotion,
   How she patiently waits through the years
For a lover who sailed on the ocean
   Whose gallant ship never appears?

Shall I tell you of hearts that are sighing
   For one kind word of comfort and cheer,
That the light from some life is fast dying
   While plighted love weeping sits near?

Shall I tell you 'tis better each duty
   Is done with a true patient hand,
Than be honored for talent or beauty
   By the proud and the great of the land?

As when on the oft-changing phases
   Of ocean, of sky, and of land,
The painter devotedly gazes,
   He pauses with pencil in hand;

So Life's varied scenes lie before me;
But when in their presence I come,
I feel their deep influence o'er me
And I stand, and shall ever stand—dumb.

A Fragment

THE weak alone are ever changing sides,
But only change as change the winds and tides;

They aimless drift upon a shoreless sea
Consistent but in inconsistency.

If we but know which way their minds are bent
We know the course of public sentiment;

As the slight vane upon the steeple shows
The points from whence the varying zephyr blows;

Saints with the pious, friends with the debased,
Each impress they receive is soon erased;

As Ocean's tide, far sweeping o'er the land,
Blots out the lines we write upon the sand;

Yet will they strive by many an artful show
To compensate for what they fail to know;

But every effort serves but to impress
Us with the force of their own littleness;

The world will value at its proper weight
Each action so diverse and complicate.

The great are simple; and we ever see
True greatness is but true simplicity.

Self-conscious of their worth, they do not feel
An innate weakness they would fain conceal;

Grand is their every deed, and grand each aim;
They seek not, yet they gain an honored name;

They rise superior to each circumstance
And prove Success lies not in Birth or Chance;

That 'tis not from without, but from within
Must come the power by which the goal we win.

What though the while some royal despot reign
And rear his golden statues on the plain!

They will not bow the head nor bend the knee,
Though flames of Persecution they may see,

Lit by the hands of Envy round them rise
All eager waiting for the sacrifice.

Such were the men who once their sails unfurled,
And turned their course unto a new-born world,

And found upon this side the stormy sea
A home from tyranny and tyrants free;

O noble heroes! Your example will
Live on increasing in its power, till

Each despot stern shall tremble on his throne,
And gloomy Bastile crumble stone by stone.

Here liberty her torch hath lit once more
That shone so dimly on the Old World's shore,

Until it seemed its feeble flickering light
Would sink into the gloom of endless Night.

Oh! may the zeal with which we guard its fires
Prove us the worthy sons of worthy sires.

.

At the Springs

A MORNING SCENE

THE sun is rising in his pride;
  The shadows fall unto the west
And veil the distant mountain-side;
  But from each glory circled crest

The mists have fled; and gladsome Day
  There sits enthroned, and sends below
His light cohorts in bright array,
  To drive afar his darksome foe.

I see the curling smoke arise
  From rustic cottage far and near;
And listening with glad surprise,
  The sounds of morning greet my ear.

The village now is all aglow
  With busy life; the tread of feet
And hum of voices come and go
  Along each narrow, winding street.

I sit within an arbor; near
  The spring is bubbling bright and pure;
The throng with mingled hope and fear
  Here turn from Art to Nature's cure.

Some seek alone relief from care,
  And coming hope to leave behind,
Within the city's stifling air,
  The troubles that oppress their mind.

Here Age, now leaning on its cane,
  Hopes to prolong its lease awhile;
And joyous Youth, still free from pain,
  With festive sports the hours beguile.

Within the shadow of a tree
  The swarthy huntsman checks his steed;
The idle crowd draw near to see
  The antlered deer, whose winged speed

Had served it well oft-times before;
  But all in vain its recent flight;
The bullet sped—its race was o'er—
  And life went out in endless night.

The stage comes rattling in amain;
  The skillful driver perched on high,
With steady hand now draws the rein,
  Nor deigns to glance at standers by.

Soon like the huntsman he shall take
  His leave of us; for year by year
The strides of Empire westward make
  More circumscribed his narrow sphere,

The race still grows more wise and weak,
  Nor skill nor learning can atone
For ills bequeathed; and oft we seek
  Surcease from evils all our own.

But here we come and live awhile,
  As lived our fathers in the days,
Ere Luxury with soothing smile,
  Had won man from Life's simple ways.

We breathe the pure fresh mountain air;
  The morning breezes fan our cheek;
Strange scenes await us everywhere,
  And Nature brings the help we seek.

At the Springs

AN EVENING SCENE

THE moon is looking down to-night
  Upon a scene as wild and weird
As ever in Time's ceaseless flight,
  To Poet's vision has appeared.

Like sentinels the mountains rise,
  And guard about our rude retreat;
While in the distance, starry skies
  With broken headlands seem to meet.

With darker hues the pines are tinged;
In softer outlines now appear
The barren rocks; the hills are fringed
With deepening shadows, grim and drear.

I look across from height to height,
While like some fair enchanted scene,
Some vision of the silent night,
Our mountain village lies between.

I see below, the people wend
Their way unto the fountain there;
While strains of music sweet ascend
Like incense on the evening air.

Some silvery voiced singer near
Delights her audience, and they own
By many an oft repeated cheer,
The power of each magic tone.

I cannot hope my simple lays
Will thus be greeted; but I wait
In silence till the coming days
Shall speak and tell me of their fate.

Independence Day—1886

 SONG to-day for all the brave,
Who in the field or on the wave,
Laid down their lives our land to save
    From foreign tyranny.

Theirs was the smoke and din of War,
The wound that left a deathless scar,
The dreary night without a star—
    To shed its brilliancy.

Ours is the golden reign of Peace,
The joy that comes when sorrows cease;
The glowing Morn whose beams increase
    In deep intensity.

They builded better than they knew;
There opened not unto their view
The glorious visions reaching through
    The centuries to be.

It is for us and ours to know
The blessings that the ages owe
To hearts and hands that struck the blow
    That gave us liberty.

And from the East, where Plymouth strand
Once saw a feeble Pilgrim band
Chant in strange accents wild and grand
    The anthems of the free;

And from the valleys of the West
By Nature's hand so richly blest,
There swells to-day from many a breast
    A joyous melody.

No party lines our land divide,
For patriotism's rising tide
Sweeps o'er the Nation far and wide
    Like a resistless sea.

And from the discord of the past,
The fife's shrill tones, the trumpet's blast,
Falls sweetly on our ears at last—
    A golden symphony.

Separation

IN joyous youth, the peasant and the peer
    Play side by side;
Nor think the barriers in some coming year
    Shall them divide.

Ere long it dawns upon their troubled gaze,
    They know not why,
There is a time to come when their pathways
    Apart must lie.

And then one goes an honored place to fill
    Beside the throne;
The other born to lowly stations, still
    Lives on unknown.

And so it was with us; in days of yore
    Our every aim
Was common; and each would not ask for more,
    Than both could claim.

But it was whispered once upon a time,
    That your pathway
Would sometime lead you on to heights sublime
    Of fairest day.

They said that by your genius you should rise
        To higher spheres ;
And even then my heart could scarce disguise
        Its gloomy fears.

For well I knew our paths would soon divide,
        And that no more
Together we would view the swelling tide
        Or silent shore.

For unto you a meaning they conveyed,
        I had not known ;
Your soul held converse with each tiny blade
        And wayside stone.

And while I walked through Nature's lighted hall
    ·   And looked in vain,
You saw the strange Handwriting on the Wall,
        And made it plain.

Beneath the sun that 'lumines all the sky
        The dim star pales ;
You shine on mountain heights afar, and I
        In lowly vales.

Jennie on the Banks of Bonnie Doon

ONE year ago I left her side,
  With many a promise to return full soon,
And claim her as my own dear bride,
  Fair Jennie on the banks of Bonnie Doon.

The hawthorn's breath perfumed the air,
  The river glowed beneath the silver moon,
The world to me seemed doubly fair,
  With Jennie on the banks of Bonnie Doon.

I sailed across the ocean wide,
  I built a home beneath the skies of June,
Yet through each passing day I sighed
  For Jennie on the banks of Bonnie Doon.

But many letters come to me,
  I read them o'er, at eve, at morn, at noon,
They tell of friends across the sea,
  And Jennie on the banks of Bonnie Doon.

I know she keeps a faithful heart,
  And I shall see her lovely form full soon,
And when we meet, no more I'll part
  From Jennie on the banks of Bonnie Doon.

Two

I SIT by the side
Of my fair young bride,
With the wealth of her bright golden tresses;
And yield me the while
To her soft loving smile
And the joy of her tender caresses.

I know in her heart
She keeps ever apart
My image with sacred devotion;
As Evening's star
Is reflected afar
In the depths of the infinite Ocean.

But dark, dreamy eyes
Before me arise,
Deep passion and sorrow revealing;
And the magical thrill
Of a voice that is still
Is silently over me stealing.

Wasted Hours

FROM sun to sun,
All tasks I shun;
My efforts are but seeming;
Each passing day
Has slipped away,
In useless, idle dreaming.

I seek my ease
Where softest breeze
Steals through the leafy bowers;
But still I find
That peace of mind
Comes not with wasted hours.

For moments slain
In doleful strain
Still tell their mournful story;
Their pale ghosts rise
Before my eyes,
And shake their tresses gory.

Fair wreaths we save
For all the brave,
Who striving, are defeated;
But none for those
Who from their foes
Ignobly have retreated.

Too late, too late,
I mourn my fate;
Stern Habit's chains have bound me;
And I have laid
The stones which made
The barriers that surround me.

And when Life's o'er,
And I before
His Presence stern am bidden,
Shame-faced I'll stand,
Within my hand,
The talent I have hidden.

Within

WHILE through the woodland's depth I strayed,
 I saw a lonely wounded bird;
But, oh! the music that it made
 Was sweeter than I e'er had heard.

And so the poet's song shall grow
 More bright amid Life's darkest hour;
As in our homes the lights will glow
 When Evening's shadows round us lower.

A Letter to my Mother

THE days have glided into weeks,
 And the weeks into months have passed,
And it has been a year to-night,
 Since I wrote to my mother last.

But when I left my dear old home,
 That home so far away,
Oh! well I know I promised then,
 I'd write her a letter each day.

And I was faithful for awhile,
And I know it gave her joy,
And brought to her careworn face a smile,
When she heard from her absent boy.

And as she looked on the dreary fields,
All wrapt in their mantles of snow,
She read in my letters of lands afar,
Where the orange blossoms blow;

Of valleys wide whose rivers glide
O'er glittering sands of gold,
And the varying seasons of the year
New beauties still unfold.

But treasures rare, and faces fair,
That I met in my wanderings here,
Drove from my fickle mind the while
The thoughts of my home so dear.

And then my letters shorter grew,
Till at length I ceased to write,
But I know it would cheer my mother's heart
To hear from her boy to-night.

So I will sit down and write to her,
And I'll beg her to forget
The pain I have caused her in the past,
And I'll say that I love her yet.

"Here's a letter, sir."   "Ah! it is from home;
   I am glad you brought it, my boy;
I hope it's good news, for, oh! to-night
   My heart is a stranger to joy."

"Dear Brother: I scarce can hold my pen;
   I have such sad words to write;
I know it will fill your heart with grief,
   For our mother died to-night.

"She had been failing for a year,
   Though the doctors did all they could;
And during the weary months she was ill,
   The neighbors were kind and good."

And she is dead.   I had not thought
   So soon from her to part;
But there's one thing doctors cannot cure,
   And that is a broken heart.

And yet I trust as she looks down
   From the glorious realms of light,
Her loving eyes will read with joy
   The letter I wrote her to-night.

The Valley of San Joaquin

H! have you seen this valley fair,
With sunlit fields and dreamy air,
And grand old pictures, quaint and rare—
    This valley of San Joaquin?

Oh! have you seen the mountains blue
That change anon to deeper hue
As if to hide from human view
    This valley of San Joaquin?

Its river like a silver thread
Glides through its narrow, winding bed;
It seems by fairies tenanted—
    This valley of San Joaquin.

All softly steals the balmy breeze
Through fragrant groves of orange trees;
With joy the wayworn traveler sees
    This valley of San Joaquin.

Like some fair gem it nestles here,
With varying hue throughout the year;
'Mid every change to me most dear—
    This valley of San Joaquin.

Remembrance

HOW welcome to our ears the songs of birds
As through the leafy woods our footsteps stray;
Like sounds of loved and dim-remembered words
They soothe our hearts and cheer our lonely way.

How sweet it is when e'er we chance to see
Within the dreary desert wastes, a flower
That sheds around its fragrance rich and free,
And holds us gently by its subtle power.

How dear to us when in a distant land
To meet with hearts that beat in unison;
To know there is a kindly helping hand
Will speed us on our way, though many shun.

And when in future years I view again
Scenes of my early youth, still held most dear,
My heart amid all change will cherish then
The memory of friendships formed while here.

A Summer Fantasy

WE may not choose our paths below,
　　Nor cross the narrow bounds
That still confine us as we go
　　Upon our daily rounds.

But visions of the far away—
　　The beautiful, the true—
Bright glimpses of a fairer day—
　　Still come to greet our view.

I breathe the city's stifled air,
　　I tread its paths of stone;
And 'mid the crowds that idly stare,
　　I walk my way alone.

As if upbuilt by magic hands,
　　Fair temples round me rise;
And treasures rare from distant lands
　　Here meet my wondering eyes.

Wealth, Beauty, Fashion walk the street;
　　Rich music greets my ear;
Each day this thought I still repeat,
　　"Man rules supremely here."

But far beyond the crowded street
  And the city's gilded domes,
I see the fields of yellow wheat,
  And the quiet country homes.

I hear the humming of the bees,
  All through the summer day;
And in the shadows of the trees,
  I see the lambs at play.

I breath again the balmy air
  That tells of fragrant flowers;
And shield me from the sunlight's glare,
  In blossom-laden bowers.

I turn to look on mountains grand,
  And valleys fair between—
But works of Art on every hand,
  Dispel the cherished scene.

Again the noise and din of Trade
  Shut out all pleasing sounds;
And I still make, as I have made,
  The city's beaten rounds.

But in my heart is a vision fair,
  And a joyous melody;
As the shell bears with it everywhere,
  The music of the Sea.

Decoration Day

TO those who fought and bravely fell
In sunny field or shady dell—
    In battle's stern array—
To those that gave their lives that we
Might be a Nation great and free—
    A tribute now we pay.

For those behind the prison bar
Who watched the conflict from afar
    And slowly pined away;
For those who died from lingering pain
And fever wasting heart and brain,
    Fair flowers we bring to-day.

For all the bravest of the land,
Entombed in Mausolèums grand,
    Where patriots homage pay,
For those who sleep in graves unknown,
Bedewed by Nature's tears alone,
    We bring the flowers of May.

She Must Not Know

I PASS her by with look so stern and cold,
  For she must ne'er my life's devotion know,
Though my fond heart her image still doth hold
  As stars are mirrored in the lakes below.

She must not know my being turns to her
  'Mid hope or fear, in shadow or in shine;
As Ocean's deepest depths the moon doth stir,
  Her presence still uplifts each thought of mine.

She is so near to me, and yet so far—
  Wealth, Beauty, Rank intrude themselves between,
E'en Genius crowned could scarcely burst the bar,
  Could Love dare scale the heights that intervene!

No, no, not in these last degenerate days
  Hath love the power it had in days of yore;
We faint, we fail—and favored Fortune sways
  Our hearts, our lives, our actions, more and more.

Yet Eros, Love divine, doth hold me still
  A willing captive; but she must not know,
Her voice, her look, can wake a deepening thrill,
  That stirs my being to its depths below.

A California Village

BESIDE this winding stream once bloomed the rose,
  Untrained. unnoticed in the distant Past ;
While on the frail wigwams of savage foes, .
  The cloud-capped mountain tops their shadows cast.

Across this fertile valley roamed the deer,
  And on its rich, luxuriant herbage fed,
Till came the strong and hardy pioneer,
  And saw a paradise before him spread.

The years have fled ; before the steady flow
  Of that vast tide that keeps its Westward way,
Have passed with lingering footsteps, sad and slow,
  The rude possessors of that bygone day.

And now a thriving village, fair to see,
  Adds grace and beauty to this ample plain—
A busy hive of human industry—
  Where through the seasons, Peace and Plenty reign.

My lot was cast within a distant state,
  Where Summer fades too soon upon the sight;
And chilling Winter comes and lingers late,
  Ere Springtime lifts from Earth her mantle white.

But here at last in western lands I've seen—
  What oft in song and story I have read—
Amid December, valleys robed in green,
  With happy warblers singing overhead.

Here Art and Nature are together blent;
  Beneath his vine and fig tree as of yore,
The husbandman may sit in sweet content,
  And feel his days of toil and hardship o'er.

I see around me lofty spires arise
  From many a house of prayer and of praise,
Still teaching us to look unto the skies,
  Whence come the blessings that have crowned our days.

And Education too, the handmaid fair,
  Of all the arts, has now her temples here,
Where youthful minds are trained with tender care,
  And formed and fitted for a higher sphere.

The sturdy blacksmith with his ringing blows,
  The preacher toiling for a better day,
The skilled physician tried and true who goes
  Through storm or sun on his unwearied way;

The busy merchant, cheerful and polite;
  The editor with quiet, careworn face,
All with a noble end and aim unite
  To bless and beautify this lovely place.

Fair as thy past has been yet fairer still,
  I trust shall be thy future; may each year
New beauty add unto each sunlit hill,
  And bring fresh joys thy lovely vales to cheer.

And when in coming days, my fancy roams
  Back o'er the weary waste of Space and Time,
I'll think of California's generous homes,
  And people bright and genial as their clime.

O Tempores, O Mores!

H! the dreary clouds of darkness,
  Oh! the anguish and the sorrow,
Oh! the want and destitution
In this land of light and freedom,
Foremost in its wealth and learning.
'Mid the pleasures of the feasting
Comes a skeleton to haunt us;
Comes and mocks us with his presence,
Driving from our hearts all gladness.
As the rift at first so tiny
In the lute, grows deep and deeper,
Till the discord in the music
Jars upon our finer feelings,
So this wail now rising upward
Mars the songs our hearts are singing.

As I musing, look about me
See the varied oppressions,
See the wrecks so sadly strewing
All the shores of Time, and listen
To the moaning of the night-wind,
Bearing seaward notes of sadness,
Surely, say I, we have fallen
On an age of deep dishonor;
Strong desire and earth-born passion
Have repressed all pure emotions;
Man is base, and from the garden
That he once so loved and cherished
Chastity's white rose has vanished,
Crushed by poisonous embraces
From rank tendrils round it twining.
As the savage warrior weareth
Trophies of his murdered victims
So his pale faced brother boasteth
Of fair hopes that he has blasted—
Of sweet faith beneath him trampled;
How again some blissful Eden
Had been entered by the serpent
And some modern Eve awakened
From the spell about her woven,
And had vainly prayed that Nature
Might in pity ever shield her
From the gaze of earth and heaven.
Well she knows that men will shun her,
Or, if seeking, drag her deeper
In the mire that lies about her.

Well she knows her sister woman
Never will forgive her weakness;
But shall welcome her betrayer
When some day he casts her from him
As a child an idle plaything
When it fails to please its fancy.
As the trained and skillful huntsman,
Seeks the wild deer and the chamois,
Knowing well their haunts and habits,
Plans and studies to entrap them,
Teaches all unto his fellows
That shall follow in his footsteps;
So have men made it their study
Ever to encompass woman
With the wiles that in all ages
Oft have been but too successful.

This is why that in our feasting
Comes a skeleton to haunt us;
This is why there is a discord
In our sweetest strains of music.
'T is because from out the garden
That men once so loved and cherished,
Chastity's white rose has vanished,
Crushed by poisonous embraces
From rude tendrils round it twining.

Loss

UPON a mountain bleak and bare,
I found a rosebush blooming fair.

I brought it from that desert place,
My pleasant valley home to grace.

I guarded it through summer days,
And shielded it from fiercest rays.

But ere the frost touched hill or dale,
I saw its crimson blossoms pale.

Nor Spring with its refreshing showers
Could e'er revive those withered flowers.

Lone, wandering, I saw one day
A humble cot beside the way.

Within its door a fair maid stood,
Just merging into womanhood.

The tender love that touched my own,
Found in her heart an answering tone.

" Oh ! come," I said, "from cottage walls
And fairer bloom in stately halls.

" Oh! come and grace a roseate bower,
Thine own sweet self the fairest flower."

When to my home I came that day,
Love smiling, lighted all the way.

There tears of Doubt and Faith's sunshine
Made its growth seem the more divine.

The years have passed; I ope to-night
A box long hidden from the light.

A faded rose is lying there
Beside a tress of golden hair.

"Ah! me," with saddened heart I say,
"Whate'er I've prized has passed away.

"I never more will love again
For highest joy brings deepest pain."

Because

AND wouldst thou ask why I'm not so
    Devoted as of yore?
And why I leave thee now to pine
    In sadness evermore?

And dost thou ask me why my love
    Hast grown so cold to thee,
Who in the long, long summers past
    Hast been so dear to me?

Then I will tell thee, maiden fair,
    Why things should thusly seem;
It is because it costs so much
    To keep thee in ice cream.

A Picture

I PRIZE all other things above,
 A picture fair;
With soft brown eyes that dream of love,
 And auburn hair.

Oh! could those lips speak now to me,
 As in past days,
'Twould be far sweeter melody
 Than worldly praise.

We walk through fragrant bowers unknown,
 With raptured eyes;
The flower that blooms for us alone
 Unnoticed dies.

But still there comes an hour to all,
 When they shall sigh
For visions fair beyond recall—
 Passed heedless by.

Oh! what to me that I have made
 Myself a name;
Too great a price is sometimes paid
 For earthly fame.

And sorrow yet would lose for me
 Its deepest stings,
But for the sweet, sad memory
 Of better things.

Not an Earthly Kingdom

WE'VE followed Thee through good report or ill
Across the hills and dales of Galilee;
Our hearts with awe and wonder, saw Thee still
The angry storm-swept sea.

We saw Thee calm amid the mighty throng,
Which moved by reverence or fiendish hate,
Had crowned Thee king, or hurried Thee along
To a blasphemer's fate.

We saw Thee burst the portals of the tomb,
Where Lazarus was laid with tender care;
We saw Thee with Thy smile dispel the gloom
That long had rested there.

We follow not for loaves and fishes; still
We know Thou comest of the kingly line;
And thousands would obey Thy royal will,
Whose hearts are wholly Thine.

And we had hoped through all these passing days,
To see Thee crush the haughty Roman's power;
But we have hoped in vain; and o'er our ways
The clouds still darkly lower.

But sometimes when we look into Thy face,
And see Thy heart oppressed with grief or care,
We think no earthly crown could ever grace
    That brow divinely fair.

And though there be no kingdom, crown, nor throne;
Though we still live 'mid unavailing strife,
We cannot leave Thee; for Thou hast alone,
    Words of Eternal Life.

Independence Day

FLING out the starry flag to-day
    And let its bright folds kiss the breeze;
Its glorious reign hath checked the sway
    Of Tyranny, o'er lands and seas.

A century hath seen it wave
    Above a Nation great and free;
Upborne by strong hands, true and brave,
    'T will wave through centuries to be.

For that which floated o'er our sires
    On Hampshire's hills and Georgia's plain,
And caught the glow of Freedom's fires.
    Their faithful sons will dare maintain.

O peaks that climb to crowns of snow!
O sunlit hills and fertile plains!
Thy sacred soil must never know
    The clanking of a despot's chains.

For yet the air is resonant
    With burning words our fathers spoke,
When with a zeal no power could daunt,
    They rose to break their galling yoke.

The grass is green where sleep the free;
    But every blade a tongue hath found
Their praise to sing; and patriots see
    An altar in each sacred mound.

And Liberty, fair Goddess, stands
    With lighted torch upon our shores;
And captives see in distant lands
    Its bright rays pierce their prison doors.

Then visions fair their sad hearts cheer;
    With joy they look on it afar
As the lone, wandering mariner
    Turns hopeful to his guiding star.

Waft gentle breeze to farthest zones
    Our songs of victory to all,
Till earth-born tyrants yield their thrones
    And Hate's dark barriers crumbling fall;

Until wherever Freedom lies
A-bleeding 'neath Oppression's blow,
Another Washington shall rise
To smite the proud Usurper low.

Awhile the soaring eagle cowered
When brethren met in deadly feud,
And the red front of Battle lowered
And wrapt the land in widowhood.

The flaming gun, the bursting shell,
The ever vengeful bayonet,
Have done their work—and done it well—
As saddened hearts remember yet.

But Nature doth her lessons teach;
Her loving hand fair flowers doth lay
Upon the lowliest grave of each
Who wore the Blue or wore the Gray.

May we her favored children own
The love a common mother shows;
Nor deign to build a Vandal's throne
Upon the wrecks of vanquished foes.

Thou who didst lead the Pilgrim bark
Across the stormy ocean wide,
Through all its devious wanderings dark,
Our Ship of State still safely guide.

Save us from storms that round us lower
  With partisan malignity;
Save us from Concentrated Power,
  And that foul fiend, dread Anarchy.

Teach us Injustice to oppose,
  Though seated on a gilded throne;
Teach us to feel another's woes,
  And make each patriot's cause our own.

Aid us against each power that's sent
  By Iron Rule to crush the free—
Or on our own broad continent,
  Or loneliest island of the sea.

We feel the thrill of newer life,
  And nobler thoughts our beings sway;
For party hate and party strife
  Evanish on our natal day.

The dark war-clouds no more appall;
  The North sends greeting to the South;
The sword hangs rusting on the wall,
  And birds build in the cannon's mouth.

By more than bands of tempered steel
  The West unto the East is bound;
Together sleep their warriors leal
  On Freedom's latest battle-ground.

And from Dakota's prairies wide
To Mexic Gulf 'neath tropic sun,
From shores wave-kissed on either side,
Swells forth the anthem—We are one.

One in each patriotic cause
That nerves to deeds of gallantry;
One in support of equal laws,
One in a common destiny.

OH! Sing Me a Song

H! sing me a song of the olden times
  When my spirit was joyous and light,
For the music sweet of its golden chimes,
  Is ringing in my heart to-night.

I have wandered far from my native home,
  And listened to the cold world's praise,
But still I sigh wherever I roam,
  For the friends of the good old days.

Then keep your music so light and gay,
  To please the fancies of the throngs
That live for the joys of the passing day
  And are charmed by its heartless songs.

But sing me a song of the long ago,
  And like the sweet harpest of Old,
You'll drive from my presence the spirit of woe
  That would wrap me in its shadowy fold.

My Bete Noir

WHO glides in through my sanctum door,
And brings a paper written o'er
A half a mile in length or more—
  Each day to show it.

Who walks the streets with vacant stare,
And seedy clothes and unkempt hair,
And lives on blasted hopes and air—
  The sad-eyed poet.

My head is aching, and my eyes
Are weary; I can scarce disguise
Each gloomy fear that doth arise—
  To him I owe it.

Will I not help his genius rise
That now is lurking in disguise
Until it soars the azure skies—
  Not if I know it.

And yet the music from that lyre
Shall grandly mount from high to higher,
For with the kindling for the fire,
  I now will stow it.

Memorial Day

GAIN we come from out our homes
    With slow and solemn tread,
To scatter flowers upon each mound
    Where sleep the patriot dead.

We bring the rose, the fairest flower
    Our mother earth can yield,
As crimson as the blood that flowed
    On many a gallant field.

We bring the drooping lily pale,
    With loving heart and hand,
An emblem of the Dove of Peace
    That hovers o'er our land.

We come to-day from far and near—
    From valley, hill and plain—
Above these sacred altars to
    Renew our pledge again,

Through all the coming years to be
    Still loyal, firm and brave,
And with our life defend the land
    These heroes died to save.

Some of us here with trembling steps,
  Remember well the day,
When those who sleep so peaceful now,
  So proudly marched away.

And oftentimes their hearts grew faint
  While watching from afar,
They saw the surging to and fro
  Of the red tide of War.

Oh! many a daring deed was done
  By gallant hearts and true,
Where the Potomac's hills of gray
  Melt into peaks of blue.

And many a maiden's rosy cheek
  Grew like the lily white,
While listening to the fearful news
  From Gettysburg's famed height.

But Georgia's plains no longer hear
  An army's conquering tread;
From Mississippi's placid breast
  The iron fleets have fled.

The thrush's piping notes displace
  The deep-toned cannon's roar;
The spirit-stirring trumpet calls
  Unto the charge no more.

Where once they met in deadly feud
  And madly staked their all,
Stern veteran's clasp each other's hands
  Across that fatal wall.

And when we see one common land
  No longer rent in twain,
Then looking on our dead, we know
  They have not died in vain.

So meeting here from year to year,
  We swear through help Divine,
The flag they loved, undimmed shall float
  Above the Palm and Pine.

When My Ship Comes In

MY ship is coming o'er the sea,
  And I wait each passing day
To catch the gleam of its snowy sails
  Through the mists of gathering spray.

It has lingered long amid the isles
  Of the dreamy tropic lands,
Where the blue waves kissed by the perfumed **breeze**
  Break on the golden sands.

But yet some day the mists shall fade,
  And the clouds will pass away ;
And my ship with its load of precious **freight**
  Shall anchor in the bay.

The visions of my childhood's hours,
  And the dreams of my later years,
Will all be realized the day
  My gallant ship appears.

The Law of Love

LET us keep amid earth's trials,
  Still a kind and gentle tone;
It may smooth some brother's pathway,
  And will light and bless our own.

Sorrows shared are sorrows lessened;
  And our tasks will lighter grow,
If we bear each other's burdens
  As we journey here below.

If we knew a word of comfort
  We might speak beside the way
Could revive some weary traveler,
  Would we hoard them day by day?

It may seem of little value,
  And we may not know while here,
That one deed we've done in kindness,
  Some sad home has filled with cheer.

But when we have reached that country
  Fairer than our hearts have known,
We shall see the golden fruitage
  Of the seeds our hands have sown.

For behind the deepest shadows,
  Falls the sunlight, full and free;
And beyond these sounds discordant,
  Floats a heaven-born melody.

A Song for the Times

WE have read in song and story
How our fathers nobly died!
Sons of Freedom! Heirs of Glory!
Have we lost their ancient pride?

Could we with prophetic vision,
All our future history trace,
Should we see these fields Elysian
Swarming with a servile race?

Should we see our schools of learning
Yield unto the pagan's shrine;
See strange incense daily burning
Where our altars stand divine?

Shall we, heirs of all the ages,
Leave this stain to coming time,
Blotting all the future pages
Of a record once sublime!

If we would not, then united
Let us now and ever stand;
And from heathen hordes benighted
We shall free our own fair land.

Bereaved

THE stars from their shining track
  Each night look down on the sea ;
But nevermore shall come back
  The light of her eyes to me.

The woods in the spring shall rejoice,
  Enrapt by the song-bird's lay ;
The low, soft tones of her voice
  Have passed from my life away.

The tide that sweeps o'er the land,
  Shall press each day on the shore ;
The thrilling touch of her hand
  I'll feel again—nevermore.

The Past

I WOULD not forget all the sorrows
   That have haunted the days of the Past;
Though oft to my eyes, unbidden they rise,
   And o'er me their dark shadows cast.

I know that its gardens have withered,
   Where my feet once delighted to stray;
But memory brings a fragrance that clings
   To its flowers more sweetly each day.

It has hopes that I hold as most precious;
   It has pleasures too sacred to share;
Some fair face I've known—a word or a tone—
   That I treasure with tenderest care.

And oft from the days of the Present,
   Whether joyful or sad they may be,
My footsteps will stray 'mid the scenes of a day
   That shall come—nevermore unto me.

For the years with their shadow or sunshine,
   Filled with quiet, or deep-stirring strife,
With darkest despair, or blessing so rare,
   Make the warp and the woof of our life.

But perhaps in the glorious Hereafter,
   Where we'll walk with unwearying feet,
Proud Victory's tones, and Defeat's crushing moans,
   Will melt into symphonies sweet.

A Golden Wedding

TWO streams that flow from sources far remote,
Upon whose surface lights and shadows float;

While odors borne upon the passing gales,
Are wafted from the blossom-laden dales;

The songs of plumaged birds from leafy bowers
Fill with sweet music swiftly fleeting hours;

The one leaps wildly in its glad career,
And gains new vigor through each passing year;

The other, soft and gentle in its flow,
Reflects the moonbeam's mild and tender glow.

At length both guided by some hidden force,
They near each other in their onward course;

And then uniting in one common tide,
Flow calmly to the ocean, far and wide.

Such were their lives; in morning far apart,
Earth's fleeting joys and sorrows filled each heart;

Her eyes first saw the light, wherein its pride
The broad Missouri rolls its turbid tide;

His, where Ohio's arrowy form glides o'er
Its pebbly bed, by fair Kentucky's shore.

Their homes were built upon the rude frontier,
Where oft the war whoop smote upon the car;

And every house a castle rude uprose
To shield its inmates from their deadly foes;

Where gentle woman, tender and refined,
In hours of need the gushing wound could bind,

Or with unerring aim speed the swift ball,
And well avenge her lord's untimely fall.

May we their children on this peaceful shore,
Where savage foemen roam the land no more,

With grateful hearts a passing tribute pay
To the brave heroes of that elder day;

Who crossed the mountains, stemmed the raging flood,
And mingled with the soil their own heart's blood;

And dying, left a priceless legacy—
The right triumphant and a nation free.

Amid such scenes their early lives were passed ;
By storms surrounded and with clouds o'ercast ;

But gaining still from trials dark and drear,
Faith, hope and courage for each coming year.

Youth brought its change—but only in degree—
More strong and brave he grew, more lovely she ;

He longed to mingle in the world of strife,
She but to grace the quiet walks of life ;

And so time passed—both feeling incomplete
Without some kindred soul their own to greet ;

And that there was, somewhere on earth a heart,
That was of each a perfect counterpart.

Such thoughts as our first father once had known,
When in the Garden fair he walked alone ;

Though vague and undefined, yet needing still,
But one on which to fix the wandering will.

Oh ! call it Fate or Fortune—what you may—
Or some strange fancy of the passing day,

Yet heart seeks heart, and soul will turn to soul,
As points the needle to the distant pole.

So flowed the current of their beings, till
They blended into one, and then each will

Was subject unto each ; and from that hour
Their lives were molded by love's gentle power.

A half a century has passed away
Since the fair dawn of that eventful day ;

A half a century of hopes and fears,
Of mutual joys and sorrows, smiles and tears ;

Of trials borne such as might well dismay
The stoutest hearts in this degenerate day ;

For soon they left the friends that they loved best
To seek their fortunes in the Golden West.

Their weary feet passed o'er that arid plain
Where through the seasons come not dew or rain ;

And from Sierra's peaks of azure hue
This land of sunshine burst upon their view ;

And here where Nature smiles with fairest face,
They found at last a humble dwelling-place.

And children came that little home to bless
And fill the measure of its happiness ;

A mother's prayers, a father's counsels, led
Them in the paths their untried feet must tread.

Then one by one they left that blest fireside,
For other homes in the great world outside;

Though many pledges came each fleeting year
Like angel-gifts from out a brighter sphere,

Yet dark or bright their lot, they gladly sought
That early home with precious memories fraught.

And once again—O father, mother dear—
We come with glad accord your hearts to cheer;

We come—but not as in the days of yore,
For care and toil our brows have furrowed o'er;

And Time will change all things below but Love,
And that is changeless as the realms above.

Yet seldom dawns on us so fair a day
But some dark shade will o'er its surface stray;

And into every earthly joy intrudes
Some sorrow that shall check our lighter moods.

For two have gone, that shall not come again;
We listen for their voices—but in vain;

And as we view our childhood's scenes to-day,
A tribute to their memory we'll pay.

For them the joys and griefs of life are o'er
And they await us on the other shore—

Bright links within the chain of endless love
That binds us to that better Home above.

But we have come, our filial love to show—
Your children as in days of long ago ;

We come while Autumn's golden tints appear,
And golden fruitage crowns the closing year,

And smiling Plenty drives dull Care away,
To celebrate your Golden Wedding Day.

Oh ! may the love that blessed that nuptial hour,
Transforming earth into a roseate bower,

Illume your pathway as you onward go,
And in Life's sunset still more brightly glow.

I Dreamed that You Loved Me

I DREAMED that you loved me;
  Your words soft and clear,
Like sweet strains of music,
  Fell on my glad ear.

Together we wandered
  The dim pathways o'er,
Renewing the pledges
  We 'd made there of yore.

We recked not the passing
  Of Time's sweeping tide;
For earth was an Eden
  With you by my side.

The soft, dreamy lovelight
  That moistened your eyes,
Was like the blue languor
  Of Orient skies.

With maidenly blushes
  Your cheeks were aglow,
Like Evening's sunset
  On mountains of snow.

I dreamed that you loved me—
The Morn's early light
Dispelled the illusion
And wrapped me in Night.

But my best hopes of heaven
I'd give, if I knew
That waking again, I
Might find that dream true.

My Mother's Gone

THAT quiet, patient face, no more—
With lines of care long furrowed o'er—
Each eve awaits me at the door—
My mother's gone.

She with a woman's tender grace,
Of every "missing link" kept trace;
Now all seems wrong about the place—
My mother's gone.

Books, papers, wildly strew the floor,
Like surf upon a storm-beat shore;
My desk with ink is spattered o'er—
My mother's gone.

My socks—one's black, the other's white;
My handkerchiefs have vanished quite;
The clock runs down 'most every night—
  My mother's gone.

The dusty pictures on the wall,
The curtains ready now to fall,
Proclaim to sundry and to all—
  My mother's gone.

Peace like a frightened dove has flown;
" From turret to foundation stone,"
John Chinaman now rules alone—
  My mother's gone.

Come back o'er mountain height and plain,
Come to this waiting heart again,
And I shall cease this sad refrain—
  My mother's gone.

🌀

I CLOSE my eyes—thy form I see ;
I sleep—'t is but to dream of thee ;

I wake—thy presence still is near ;
I listen—'t is thy voice I hear.

The rosebud's deepest hues but speak
The blushes that suffuse thy cheek ;

Italian skies are overhead ;
I see thy soft blue eyes instead.

The tints of harvest I compare
To the bright radiance of thy hair ;

In the vast Ocean's depths I see
An emblem of my love for thee.

The winds that kiss thy lips to-day
A message from my heart convey ;

And though the plains may us divide,
And mountains rise thy form to hide,

Yet all that's fair to hear or see,
Bring to me visions blest of thee.

Rest

I'T was night on Galilee,
   And the winds blew loud and shrill,
When across the stormy sea
   Came the accents, '' Peace, be still.''

Then the waves that lashed the shore
   Sunk into a quiet rest,
As the child, when griefs are o'er,
   Sleeps upon its mother's breast.

I am sailing o'er Life's sea,
   And the storms are rude and chill;
Clouds are lowering gloomily,
   Savior, speak now, " Peace, be still.''

In the Mountains

FAR separated from the busy throng
  That strive and toil through the long summer hours,
I musing, listen to the happy song
Of tuneful choirs hid in the leafy bowers.

Yon pathway climbing up the mountain side,
  Half hid by towering pines and fringed with flowers,
Leads outward to the fertile valleys wide,
  Into another, larger world than ours;

But not more fair; though man no temple rears
  With gilded domes and long drawn aisles, wherein
The humble worshiper entrancèd hears
  The prayers that ease him of his guilt and sin;

Here Nature's open book before him lies;
  And Nature's voices hymned to one sweet tune—
The glad green earth, the soft blue summer skies—
  The hope and promise of the days of June—

All these uplift him to a higher plane,
  And melt his heart, until there steals within
His soul an earnest longing to attain
  To something better than he yet has been.

The breezes bring sweet odors from afar;
    The while through all my veins there gently thrills
A newer life; and Hope like a bright star,
    Shines kindly on me o'er the purple hills.

At last the old-time shackles, that so long
    Held me in their half-fatal thrall, and made
My chosen life-work fail and marred my song,
    With the dark relics of the Past are laid.

As priests and prophets of the ancient days,
    Turned from the city with its toil and strife,
And for a season treading lonely ways,
    Prepared for the great mission of their life;

So here alone, save for some choice book culled
    From favorite authors, that suggests a theme
For deepest thought, I feel my senses lulled
    To calmer moods, by voice of wood and stream.

And thus by meditation I may know
    My own heart better, and can trace the course
Of all my secret thoughts and deeds, and go
    Through all their devious wanderings to their source;

And knowing well my heart, I hold the key
    That will strange mysteries to me unlock;
As living waters poured forth full and free
    When Israel's leader smote the desert rock.

In the City

THE happy throngs here pass me by—
  The young, the gray, the witty;
Fair visions greet my wondering eye
  In the heart of the mighty city.

They've heard the call from East and West,
  By flood and fire invaded;
Their names shall evermore be blessed
  By hearts that their hands have aided.

No voice responds unto my own—
  No tender throb of pity;
Who cares if I should die alone
  In the heart of the mighty city!

Parted

S HE came and all was light;
She went and all was night;
  For a joy when past
  Is a grief at last
That mocks us with our woe.

Oh! some are dear to me
Beside this Western Sea,
  But the one fair face
  With its nameless grace
Will rise where'er I go.

The arid plains divide
Me from my joy and pride,
  And the mountains rise
  To the vaulted skies
To hide her from my view.

But in the winds that blow,
Her voice comes, soft and low,
  And where'er I roam,
  In the azure dome
I see her eyes of blue.

Purified

DENYING self alone we rise;
 Life's crosses we must daily bear
If in fair realms beyond the skies
 Bright crowns unfading we would wear.

How oft we see some cherished hope
 To sadness and despair give way,
While we in doubt and darkness grope,
 Too crushed to moan, too proud to pray.

But let us not bewail our fate,
 Nor sigh because of seeming loss;
By fiery trials we separate
 From precious gold the worthless dross.

And so He tries us day by day,
 And with a chastening hand He drives
The base and sordid parts away;
 It is our better self survives.

We press our hand upon the strings
 And they give forth a sweeter sound
We crush the rosebud and it flings
 Its fragrant odors far around.

The Master knows our every heart;
 He knows the fairest melody
It can produce; and with an art
 Divine, He touches every key.

Mists

I STAND upon a mountain's lofty height;
   A heavy veil hangs o'er the depths below;
And by its darkened folds it hides from sight,
   The purple vineyards and the brooklet's flow;

The orchards pendent with their luscious fruit,
   The yellow stubble where the young quails call,
The tasseled corn, like soldiers stern and mute,
   The jasmine climbing o'er the cottage wall.

Lo! from his quiver now, the King of Day
   Speeds his swift arrows tipped with golden light,
Dispensing warmth and beauty on their way,
   And driving all the mists of morn to flight.

So oft in life the gathering clouds hang o'er
   Our pathway here; but through each day we know,
The deepest gloom will fade His smile before,
   And all the world with joyous sunshine glow.

Autumn Leaves

SEE before me now a beauteous bloom
Of autumn leaves; a deep embroidery,
Wrought by fair hands that were so dear to me;
It leads my wandering thoughts to that dim room,

Wherein she sat and with meek patience wove,
The while the hours wing-footed past us flew,
Their warp and woof with many a golden hue;
While I, with sad forebodings, vainly strove

To drive afar thoughts that would intervene;
For well I knew that soon we two must part,
And that the web that bound us heart to heart
Would severed be; and this sweet, blissful scene

Become a precious memory of the Past.
Oh, ruthless hand of Time! it oft destroys
Our fairy castles; and for present joys
Leaves a deep sorrow which through life shall last.

But not the pleasures of the passing day,
The light of smiling eyes, the tender grace
Of woman's changeful moods can e'er displace
That love which holds me in its gentle sway.

My joys have faded ; like the autumn leaves,
  That drift adown the vale before the breeze,
  They darkling lie; but Hope a spring-time sees
And Faith a never-fading garland weaves.

A Summer Scene

THROUGH my window there floats to-day,
  The odor from new-mown fields of hay.

A bird is singing in yonder tree
Its self-taught notes of ecstasy.

The honest watchdog barks amain
At the traveler in the dusty lane.

I hear the far, faint hum of bees
That gather sweets from blossoming trees.

In the distance the village lies,
Glowing 'neath the molten skies.

The din and noise of its busy street,
Die ere they reach my far retreat.

Beneath the fig tree's ample sway
The merry feet of childhood stray ;

Soon shall they leave their calm abode
To walk in Life's hard-beaten road.

The winds that breathe on hill and plain,
Sway the broad fields of yellow grain.

I see the toilers in sun and shade
March to the sound of the reaper's blade.

They have found a far more precious mine
Than the Argonauts of " Forty Nine."

Where rise yon circling wreaths of smoke,
Shielded by clusters of massive oak,

From the hot noonday's heat and glare,
Is a country mansion, tall and fair.

And where the roses white and red,
On the balmy air their fragrance shed,

And lingering sunbeams love to play,
A humble cot stands by the way.

The Iron Horse with flaming eye
And piercing neigh, sweeps grandly by,

Drawing the richly laden car
Of grain and fruits to lands afar ;

And dwellers in some sister state,
Where dreary winter lingers late,

Shall bless these shores where Plenty stands
And scatters gifts with lavish hands.

Like the liquid depths of a maiden's eyes.
Is the vaulted dome of the azure skies;

One silvery cloud appears to view,
Like a sail afloat on the ocean blue.

Wrapt in shadows, solemn and grand,
Far to the North, the lone Buttes stand;

They rise before me in dim outline,
Like castles old on the dreamy Rhine.

Along the purple eastern skies,
Sierra's snow-crowned peaks arise;

Beneath the sun's fierce glare they lie
Like a shaft of light athwart the sky.

A pale mist half conceals each crest
Of the mountain range upon the west;

But nearer and clearer stretch away
The hills of gold and the hills of gray.

The slanting rays of light now fall
On vines that cling to roof and wall.

The sun sinks slowly to his rest
Like a tired child on its mother's breast.

Night gathers round me, calm, serene,
And darkness veils the rural scene.

But still an impress has been made
That never from my heart shall fade;

And when o'er mountain height and plain
Within my home I stand again,

A vision fair shall come to me,
Of lands beside the Western Sea,

Where peaks begirt with crowns of snow
Look down on sun-kissed vales below;

And music sweet from these fair climes
Shall mingle in my after-rhymes.

A Lesson

I AM sitting fondly poring o'er a volume quaint and old,
On whose pages. truest sages, all their inmost thoughts unfold.

And they tell of heavy crosses, of the loss of earthly gain;
Of sweet friendship changed to hatred, pleasure turned to
lingering pain.

And one paints a fairy picture, with sweet hope and patience
rife,
Of the love and the devotion of an earnest, faithful wife.

Tells of vows by him unplighted, tells of bliss to him unknown;
Sings of mutual joys and sorrows, while he goes through life alone.

And another sings so sweetly as his footsteps sadly roam,
Sings the song of every nation, for it is of Home, Sweet Home.

Not for him its rest is given, not for him its bright fires burn;
Not for him loved hands shall open wide the door for his return;

But he walks past glowing windows, sees a haven fair inside;
Sees the good wife's smiling features, sees the husband's look
of pride.

Not the one that's blest with treasures rarest that the world can
hold,
But the wanderer gazing on them, of their precious worth has
told.

As the wife that long has waited for a blessing still denied,
Sees in dreams a form of beauty nestling fondly to her side;

Feels a warm breath on her bosom, feels a joy a mother knows
Hears an infant's tender wailing, that still faint and fainter
grows:

So I reach out in the darkness for a hand that seemeth near;
Listen for a gentle footstep—sweetest music to my ear.

From my hand the book has fallen, and I silent—dream alone;
While I feel the loss so deeply of a love I ne'er have known.

Vacation Musings

Read before the YOLO COUNTY TEACHERS' INSTITUTE, at the Woodland
Opera House, Thursday Eve, November 22, 1888.

THE narrow walls we leave behind—
   The daily paths our feet have trod—
   For vaulted dome and yielding sod,
And wider ranges of the mind.

We dreaming lie 'neath Summer skies,
   Beside a brook whose waters flow
   From mountains crowned with virgin snow,
That dimly in the distance rise.

From branch to branch the squirrels spring;
   The birds sing sweetly overhead;
   While round us and beneath are spread
Fair Nature's richest carpeting.

The West-wind sways the stately firs,
   And their soft music, sad and low,
   Like echoes of the long ago,
The current of our being stirs.

From out the wreck of yesterdays
.   Another Argosy we freight,
   And sail beyond the narrow strait,
Past headlands bold and sheltered bays;

Nor deem our wanderings shall cease,
O'er strange, fair lands or boundless main,
Till homeward we return again,
- And bear with us the Golden Fleece.

Again we dream the dreams of Youth;
Again we gird our armor on,
And march forth in Life's rosy dawn
To battle bravely for the Truth.

Our hearts are true, our faith is strong,
And full of cheer the songs we sing;
Another David with his sling
To bring to earth the giant Wrong.

No more with halting steps we climb,
By slow degrees, from height to height;
But reach at once by sudden flight
The topmost summits of our time.

Nor through the process of the years,
The ripening harvest we await,
That once we deemed came all too late
From seeds we sowed 'mid doubts and fears.

No more withheld the guerdon meet
For toiling hands and wearied brain,
And hearts that soothe the pangs of Pain,
Until Life's journey is complete.

The shadows fade ; dark discords cease ;
  Falls on our ears a silvery chime ;
  And full and free the hand of Time
Rings in the thousand years of Peace.

The gloomy Bastile overthrown,
  The crumbling crown, the broken chain,
  And Freedom's universal reign,
For sad Sarmatia's tears atone.

As when we gladly turn one day
  From distant lands to childhood's scenes,
  Across each league that intervenes,
We slowly trace the lengthening way.

Expectant Hope, fleet as the light
  From orbs that 'lume the distant spheres,
  Flies to each spot of former years,
And paints for us her pictures bright.

Again the old homestead we see ;
  Again upon its threshold stand,
  And each warm pressure of the hand
Awakes some fondest memory.

But Fancy lays her wand aside,
  And Reason stern resumes her sway ;
  Before our view stretch far away,
Snow-mantled peaks and deserts wide.

Our thought a winged Mercury, soars
Untrammeled by the touch of clay,
Beyond the purple Gates of Day,
To fairest climes and farthest shores.

Firm-paced and slow, our deeds move on ;
Though resting on the dumb cold ground,
Like towering peaks they rise sun-crowned,
And meet and greet the coming dawn.

O magic Thought! Creative Power!
That filled with worlds unmeasured space,
And spoke to life a new-born race,—
Still potent in the present hour.

Or gentle as the zephyr's sigh,
Or leaping forth in words of fire
That voice a nation's deep desire,
And wake to deeds that never die.

Still Homer's deathless lays enshrine
Great Agamemnon's victories ;
The lightnings of Demosthenes,
Each tyrant fears as wrath divine.

Nor less, nor more deserving praise,
He in whose fertile brain is wrought
Fair pictures, touched by subtle thought,
That cheer us 'mid Life's dusty ways,

Than he, whose dauntless spirit leads
  To unknown lands beyond the sea,
  Where a great nation yet to be,
Shall light the world with noble deeds.

And as the years shall circle on,
  Each patriot strikes with truer aim,
  While thinking on the cherished name
Of Leuctra or of Marathon.

The past still in the present lives;
  Each force in all the ages gone,
  Though still unseen, is moving on,
And to our lives its impress gives.

Yon peaks that 'mid the silence reign
  Were slow-evolved from mother earth;
  Nor rose full-armed in sudden birth,
As Pallas sprang from Zeus's brain.

We leave behind the purling stream,
  The mountain pathway, cool and sweet,
  For the great city's crowded street,
Where white sails in the harbor gleam.

On pleasure bent, glide to and fro,
  The sons of Luxury and Ease;
  And Fashion's foolish votaries
Sweep by pale forms of Want and Woe.

Here rarest works of Art we see;
Here Science rears her lofty fane;
And Poverty pleads not in vain
To open-hearted Charity.

There is a welcome in the air;
A greeting in the outstretched hand;
To-day another honored band
Our hearts and homes shall freely share.

These bear aloft no banner rent
In battlestorm by shot and shell,
But pale and careworn faces tell
Of years in faithful service spent.

The Nation crowns each gallant deed
Of all that host of freemen brave,
Who in the field, or on the wave,
Have served her in her hour of need.

And is it near, or is it far,
When we shall own with royal will,
That smiling Peace hath heroes still
As worthy as grim-visaged War?

'Tis meet where side by side have wrought,
True sons from lands of Palm or Pine,
A laurel wreath their hands should twine,
Alike for men of Deed or Thought.

That we should teach unto mankind
  Our chosen creed: " We prize far more
  Than fabled wealth of golden ore,
The treasures of the heart and mind."

We stand the heirs of every age ;
  For us Canova's chisel wrought,
  And myriad-minded Shakspeare's thought
Was breathed upon the living page.

The Galileos in their cells
  For us survey the universe ;
  And Nature like a kindly nurse,
To them her prisoned secrets tells.

For us a brighter hope was born ;
  For us the martyr's blood was shed ;
  And hours of darkness and of dread
Were preludes to the coming morn.

To these fair lands beside the sea,
  Bold pioneers have cleaved the way,
  And builded for a better day,   .
And greater opportunity.

Land of my childood's dreams! On thee
  Italia's deep blue skies look down,
  And purple grapes of Eschol crown
Thy sunlit vales of Thessaly.

Still brighter lead thy guiding star!
Until the tides that Westward sweep,
And to these shores their progress keep,
Converging here from realms afar,

Into one common current draw,   .
The Ancient Hebrew's cultured heart,
Hellenic love of Lore and Art,
And Roman fealty to Law.

Beyond my eager gaze recedes
Each picture touched by Fancy's glow ;
Stern Duty calls me and I go
From dreaming thoughts to waking deeds.

Epigrams

Epitaph on Bismarck.

HERE lies the Iron Chancellor;
　While here on earth, although a
Prince with realms within his grasp,
He still sighed for Samoa.

Is Marriage a Failure?

"THIS is a question," says the sage,
　"That's ever wrapt in doubt;
Since those who're out wish to get in,
And those in, to get out."

Her Reply

"MY dear, have you seen my last poem?"
　I said, with a feeling of pride,
As I passed her the half-open paper,
"I hope so," she softly replied.

The Valley of Capay

COME with me where nature fair
Shows a mother's fondest care ;
Through the seasons of the year,
Filling homes with joy and cheer;
Where the lights and shadows play
O'er the Valley of Capay.

Orchards dotting hill and plain,
Purple vineyards, waving grain ;
Breezes laden with perfumes
Of the fragrant orange blooms,
Greet us while our footsteps stray
Through the Valley of Capay.

Music through the sunny hours,
Songs of birds in leafy bowers ;
Rural scenes that charm the view,
Mountains changeful in their hue ;
These beguile the passing day
In the Valley of Capay.

Here the sunbeams softly gleam
On the bosom of a stream,
That its winding way doth take
From a calm and placid lake ;
Brooklets flow and fountains play
In the Valley of Capay.

Here I fain would spend my days;
Here I'd sing my sweetest lays;
Here would end my latest quest
With the friends that I love best,
Never 'mid the years to stray
From the Valley of Capay.

After the War

THEY had gradually gathered together
Those veterans grim and gray;
And many a scar from the cruel war
They'd carried with them away.

Some there had fought with General Grant
And some with General Leo;
And some had been with Sherman
In his famous March to the Sea.

Oh! many a savage fray they'd seen
Upon the South-land Plain;
And as they drained their glasses
They fought them o'er again.

But as they talked of battles past,
　Fought by brave hearts and true,
The fire of Hate gone out of late,
　Began to burn anew.

Then far in a corner rose a man,
　He was old and gray and bent;
His clothes were all torn and tattered,
　And on a cane he leant.

Said he: " I've stood for many an hour
　Where the shot fell thick and fast;
But the cruel War is over;
　Let the Past now be the Past."

Then came those veterans round him
　And tearful, grasped his hand;
And said: " You've spoken sir, aright;
　'T will be as you command."

And they drank his health together
　And his eyes grew glad and bright,
As the ruddy drops of wine out poured
　Like blood in a deadly fight.

At last said one: " Please tell, old man,
　Where you got those gallant scars?
For we know you've many a tale to tell
　Of long and cruel wars.

"Was it at Vicksburg's long-drawn siege,
　Or on Antietam's plain;
Or where Lee's veterans scaled the heights
　Of Gettysburg in vain?"

The old man answered; and his look
　Was sad and far away;
"In the shot tower at St. Louis
　I've worked for many a day."

To an Absent One

LONELY am I to-day.
For thou art far away,
Gone like a silver ray
    From my rapt vision ;
Happiest was I of men,
Love smiled upon me then,
Sadly I turn again
    From fields Elysian.

Swiftly the moments glide
While sitting by thy side,
Heaven is opened wide
    When thou art nearest ;
Come to this waiting heart,
Never on earth to part—
Truest of all thou art—
    Fondest and dearest.

Now thou no more art nigh,
Sadly the breezes sigh
For the dear days gone by,
    And thy bright laughter ;
But to my far retreat
Comes there a courier fleet,
Bringing a promise sweet
    Of the Hereafter.

My Love

HER eyes are like the June skies,
　　Her hair like waves of light;
Her dimpled cheek a dainty bunch
　　Of roses, red and white.

The clink of yellow treasures
　　The miser loves to hear;
The music of her laughter
　　Alone can charm my ear.

She meets me in the doorway,
　　Her fair face wreathed in smiles;
And with her arts bewitching
　　The evening hours beguiles.

I come and sit beside her
　　And with her ringlets play;
I kiss her and caress her
　　And she does not say me nay.

Oh! what a joy I deem it,
　　Her fairy form to hold—
She is my sister's baby
　　And only twelve months old.

A Mother's Kiss

THE Day its oriflamme of light has furled;
The wing of Night has drooped above the world;

Around the hearth we come with love and cheer,
Nor gathering clouds nor threatening storms we fear;

Some innocent amusement free from guile,
Serves for a time the passing hours to while;

In study then the moments pass from view,
Till evening prayers are said with reverence due;

Then like the bird that seeks the sheltering nest,
Each weary careworn heart prepares for rest;

The little ones retire with movements slow,
To downy beds; the lights burn dim and low;

When a sweet voice breaks on the silence deep,
" Come kiss me, mother, ere I go to sleep."

The mother stoops to where her darling lies
In darkened room, with eager-waiting eyes,

And smoothing back from that young brow so fair,
With loving hands, its curls of auburn hair,

Gives to her child a mother's fondest kiss,
That fills its tender heart with purest bliss;

Till gently soothed beneath that warm impress,
It sinks to sleep and dreams of happiness.

What wonder if it sweetly sleep to-night!
Or if its face be radiant with light!

Or if it softly speak as though it heard
Sweet music like the carol of a bird!

Or sees some heavenly vision! For I know
I saw them, too, so many years ago;

And though so long, I well remember this—
They followed close upon my mother's kiss.

Though we are many miles apart to night,
Her face still rises to my tear-dimmed sight;

I see her as I saw her, years ago,
With bending form and footsteps sad and slow,

And turning to her, say through shadows deep,
"Come kiss me, mother, ere I go to sleep."

For through the night's dark shades I sadly miss
The lingering fragrance of a mother's kiss.

L'Envoi

'TIS something to have sailed bright streams
  Though beyond the billows are breaking;
'T is something to have dreamed fair dreams
  Though they end in a sad awaking.

The gains and losses of To-day
  Are the memories of To-morrow;
And sweet as the joys that light our way
  Are the somber shades of sorrow.

Go little book—each line inwrought
  With my heart's best distillation;
And whether you are shunned or sought
  I have had my compensation.